𝒟

Bride of the
Morning Star

W

Bride of the Morning Star

»» »» »» »» »» »» »» »» »» »» »» »»

DON COLDSMITH

DD

A Double D Western
Doubleday
NEW YORK   LONDON   TORONTO   SYDNEY   AUCKLAND

A DOUBLE D WESTERN
PUBLISHED BY DOUBLEDAY
a division of Bantam Doubleday Dell Publishing Group, Inc.
666 Fifth Avenue, New York, New York 10103

A DOUBLE D WESTERN, DOUBLEDAY,
and the portrayal of the letters DD
are trademarks of Doubleday, a division of
Bantam Doubleday Dell Publishing Group, Inc.

Library of Congress Cataloging-in-Publication Data

Coldsmith, Don, 1926–
Bride of the morning star / Don Coldsmith.—1st ed.
    p.   cm.—(A Double D western)
    1. Indians of North America—Great Plains—Fiction. I. Title.
PS3553.O445B7   1991
813'.54—dc20   91-11275
CIP

ISBN 0-385-26303-1
Copyright © 1991 by Don Coldsmith
All Rights Reserved
Printed in the United States of America
November 1991
First Edition

Author's Note
» » »

The ceremony of the Morning Star practiced by the Pawnees is one of those odd exceptions to the usual, but it is real. I wanted to depict it through the eyes of an adopted member of the Pawnee nation, one who is not quite able to accept its basic premise. Bear Paws, formerly Strong Bow of the People, is a character from the previous book, *Return of the Spanish*. He is living with his wife's people, the Pawnees, which gives him the perspective I wanted for the Morning Star story.

As the research developed, I happened to learn of a very similar historical incident, which seems well documented. A captive Piegan girl of the southern Blackfeet was rescued by her people, after her captors, the Wolf band of the Pawnees, had actually begun the final ceremony to the Morning Star. That story is retold by James Willard Schultz in his book *Blackfeet and Buffalo*. It was told to him by Charles Rivois, an adopted Piegan, who was a participant in the rescue. While some of the circumstances are similar, this book is not intended to depict that event. It is worthy of note that in Rivois' account, the rescued girl did appear to have been subjected to a hypnotic influence, as I have indicated in our story. His description is quite suggestive of a "deprogramming" of the captive after her rescue.

The rescue of the Piegan girl, Lance Woman, took place in 1856, and is said to be the last attempt to carry out the traditional Pawnee sacrifice to the Morning Star.

DON COLDSMITH

Time Period: 1725

Bride of the
Morning Star

1
» » »

Bear Paws sat in the front row of spectators, trying hard not to let his trembling be apparent to the others. The darkness of pre-dawn was cool, but he was sweating. Only a little time, now, until the sign would appear. There was a hush, an excited anticipation.

He touched the knife at his waist with moist fingers, making sure that it was ready. Soon, the red Morning Star would look over Earth's eastern rim, and the events of the day would be set in motion. His life could never be the same again. At best, he would lose his home, his wife and family. Possibly, his life. But this was something that he must do, or die in the attempt. He had come to believe that this was his purpose for being here, his quest. Not until this spring, in the Moon of Awakening, had he realized it. His mind roved back . . . four, no . . . five seasons ago.

It was not a vision, or any such spirit-visitation that had started this bizarre series of events. Looking back, however, he could see that it had been a number of improbable occurrences. Each, by itself, seemed to mean nothing. Together . . . *aiee!* He traced the sequence in his memory. Any one of the events that had led to this point, had it not happened, would have made this rescue impossible. Maybe it still was.

Strange, he thought. *Just when one thinks he understands the way of things . . . Never can one know what lies ahead.*

He had agreed to spend the summer, that fateful summer of five seasons ago, guiding the Spanish. It had appeared to be a pleasant interlude, seeing new country, learning of new customs to the north, acting as hand-sign interpreter. He had been young and foolish, and angry with his parents. They had objected to his plan. So did his older brother, the respected holy man. Red Horse had advised against it. But nobody could understand, he thought. A late child, the child of a couple's older years, is not allowed to grow up. The objections of his family made him all the more determined. In the way of a young man who, in the prime of his young manhood, knows everything, he had gone, anyway. A foolish thing.

There had been cause to regret his decision. The Spanish party had been massacred here on the Platte, as the French traders now called this river. Not by French, whom they had sought, but by the Pawnee, known to his own tribe as the Horn People. He had been captured, and had fully expected to be tortured and killed.

But . . . another strange coincidence. Pretty Sky, the beautiful girl who was now his wife, had intervened. It had not been easy, for there were those who sought vengeance on him. Gradually he had been accepted, virtually adopted into the tribe.

And gradually, the charms of Pretty Sky had made him forget, or at least postpone, the idea of returning to his own People in the Tallgrass Hills. He felt some regret that his parents would now think him dead. He would go to see them some day. But that day had been postponed. Pretty Sky discovered that she was pregnant. A small son joined them, and it was good. Two seasons later, a daughter, and that, too, was good.

Meanwhile, Bear Paws was gaining respect among his wife's people. His skill as a horseman and hunter brought admiration and friendship from the other men. Red Hand, who had once vowed to kill him, was now his trusted friend. The Pawnees were acquiring more horses, and a man with knowledge of their use was valuable.

Thus, Bear Paws felt useful, appreciated, loved, and quite comfortable among his adopted people. Using hand-signs at first, he had mastered the use of the Pawnee tongue. He dressed as they did, and his horn-shaped scalp-lock jutted from the top of his shaved head like that of any other man of the Horn People.

It had taken much time to understand some of their customs. Among his own people, the one big celebration of the year was the Sun Dance. The entire nation gathered each year in the Moon of Roses . . . early summer . . . to celebrate the return of the Sun, after its light had threatened to fade out entirely. Now the Moon of Long Nights and the Moon of Snows were conquered, left behind in the glory of the Sun's renewal. This regained power caused in turn the return of the grass, the buffalo, and the vibrant energy of the People. Their lives depended upon this cycle each season. The week-long ceremony of the Sun Dance was a thing of joy, a celebration. There was feasting, dancing, and visiting with friends and relatives from other bands. But there were also prayers of thanksgiving, of supplication, vows pledged, and sacrifices in honor of favors granted or pledges fulfilled.

Then each band would go its separate way, to meet again in the Moon of Roses next year, at a new site.

Here, among his wife's people, the ceremonies were much more complicated. Theirs was an odd mixture, by the standards of Bear Paws' own people, who were hunters. These were growers, living in permanent villages of earth-lodges, planting large crops of corn, beans, and pumpkins. But in addition, there was also the Summer Hunt. After the second hoeing of the corn, the fields were left abandoned for a time as the entire village moved out onto the grassland to hunt buffalo.

This was the season that Bear Paws enjoyed most. It was almost like the thrill of the hunt among his own people. Yes, he admitted freely that he hated the hoeing of the crops, hated the feel of the hoe handle as he swung it, chopping weeds that threatened the corn. He had grown up seeing the shoulder blades of buffalo, had gnawed meat from quite a few. Not until he had used such a bone, lashed to a stick with rawhide to fashion a hoe, had he really developed a dislike for this portion of a buffalo's anatomy. It was much better to hunt them, and the Summer Hunt provided this opportunity.

It was in his second or third season here, however, that he began to realize the complicated variety of ceremonials and special occasions celebrated by these, his wife's people. There were a great number of these, celebrating various phases of the seasons. Not only Sun's activities, but those of Moon. She was the wife of Sun, Pretty Sky told him.

Many of the other heavenly bodies also played an

important role in the ceremonies. The timing of these occasions seemed quite mysterious. No one really knew when to expect them, except in general terms. Announcement was made as the time approached, by the appropriate holy man. There were many of these, too. A separate priest for each heavenly entity: Morning Star Priest, Evening Star, other priests whose function was not so clear. The main duty of some was to be the keeper of one of the sacred bundles. There were several of these, with purposes that seemed rather vague to the outsider, Bear Paws. Some were dedicated to the four directions, though not the same four with which he was familiar. East was important, of course. Lodge doors faced east, as among his own people. But the bundles were dedicated to Northeast, Northwest, Southeast, and Southwest. This had been very confusing to him. There was one bundle that he had never seen used, called the Skull Bundle. He was not certain that he wanted to know why, but eventually learned.

It was part of their Creation Story. A great holy man, one of the first to enter the world, had given the Horn People this bundle. He had directed that at his death his skull be tied to the bundle to distinguish it from a similar medicine-bundle, the Morning Star Bundle. Thus it had come down through the ages. Of course, Pretty Sky assured him, this was not the original skull. It had been replaced from time to time as the old one became dilapidated. It gave him a creepy feeling. In light of later events, it may have been a premonition, a warning.

Still, life was good. Sky was a devoted wife, and their children were fat and happy. It was easy to delay any thoughts of returning to the prairies of his people, even to visit. Each season, it became easier, as he settled into the routine of this strange life.

There had come a few horse-stealing raids by an enemy to the north. Bear Paws was not certain what nation was involved, because he did not know what name for them his own people used. Probably, it was a tribe with whom his own Elk-dog People had had little contact. The hand-sign used by his adopted people was merely "Enemy."

He had been active in the pursuit and recovery of the horses. In the skirmish with the enemy, he had accounted for one warrior in a manner that had brought him much prestige. The other was a big man, apparently a sub-chief or leader of some sort. He was mounted on a powerful black horse, and was swinging a long-handled stone ax. It was difficult to stand his ground against such a charge, but Bear Paws managed to draw an arrow to its head and loose it directly into the painted chest. Actually, it would have been much more dangerous to try to run. But, those who saw the event were impressed with Bear Paws' bravery, and told and retold the story many times.

His friend Red Hand took the scalp and brought it to him to decorate his bow case. Someone else caught the black horse, which became Bear Paws' prize of battle. The adopted warrior from the prairie was well on his way to prestige as a man of the Horn People.

Then, two seasons ago, the fortunes of the band had seemed to turn. A horse raid by the Enemy had been successful. A small raid, to be sure. The loss was no more than twenty animals, but it was a matter of principle. The recovery party, including Bear Paws, tracked the horse thieves for three days, and then lost the trail. There were arguments over whose fault that was, but they were never resolved. The loss was more in prestige than in horses.

It was the same summer that they returned from the

Summer Hunt to find that a herd of elk had browsed their way through the fields, eating corn, knocking down more, and trampling pumpkins. By means of much extra work on an emergency basis, they were able to salvage barely enough for winter survival and for seed.

The next season came a drought. The corn sprouted poorly, grew in a spindly fashion with poor root systems, and it appeared that the harvest would be very scant. They must rely heavily on the Summer Hunt.

But that, too, was poor. The same drought that had already withered the crops had hit the grasses, also. With little to eat in this area, the buffalo had gone somewhere else. The animals were few and far between, and those they managed to kill were thin and stringy. The situation was beginning to appear desperate.

Bear Paws remembered a season or two when the People had encountered such problems. They had simply taken down the lodges and moved elsewhere. For the Horn People, this was not an option. Their earthlodges, their village, their fields could not be moved. They must stay here, and weather out the difficulty.

There was much talk, but little else, and the leaders seemed to be waiting for something. A vision, perhaps? Bear Paws longed to ask, but sensed that this was a thing which he should not do.

It was in the Moon of Falling Leaves that the Morning Star Priest made the announcement.

"Morning Star is displeased. We have neglected Him, my brothers. Now, it is time for a vision. Let us make ourselves ready, open our spirits to His. Whoever is chosen, let him come to me and speak."

There was a murmur in the circle. Its tone said that there was something very important here. More important, it seemed to Bear Paws, than the holy man's words warranted. He had been expecting an announcement of a plan of some sort. This was the entire tone of the gathering at the council fire that night, and he had expected a major announcement.

Instead, this . . . this *nothing.* "We must all wait for somebody to have a vision . . ." Bear Paws was close to disgust as he walked back to the earth-lodge that he and Pretty Sky shared with her family.

His own reaction was so intense that he overlooked the fact that no one was talking. There was a hushed silence through the village, a reverence, almost. He had no way of knowing that for this village this had been the most momentous announcement that they could ever have heard.

Likewise, there was no way for him to know its far-reaching effect on his own life, and that of the Elk-dog People.

2
» » »

"Sky, tell me of the vision that they seek," Bear Paws requested.

"What do you mean?" Pretty Sky asked.

Her husband looked at her quizzically.

"The announcement . . . old Hawk's Tail . . . *aiee*, you were there, Sky. He talked of the Morning Star, and that everyone should look for a vision."

"Yes. He is the Morning Star Priest."

"But this . . . I have been with you five seasons now, and this has never been spoken of."

"Yes, that is true. But of course, we have seldom had such a run of misfortune."

Pretty Sky realized that she was being evasive. She hated to do that. Bear Paws had been a good husband, and had adapted well to the ways of her people. Some of their customs must have seemed strange to him. She would never forget his indignation when their friend Reed Woman became romantically involved with her husband's younger brother. To Bear Paws, it was scandalous.

"But that is in the family," she had tried to explain. "It is her choice."

"She will leave her husband, then?" Bear Paws asked.

"No, no. Only for this month."

"This *month?*"

"Yes. She cannot be with her husband this month."

"Cannot be?"

Pretty Sky sighed deeply.

"Look, Bear, you know that my people trace their family through the woman's side?"

"Yes, of course. Many nations do."

"So . . . all her children are hers, but may have a different father. It is her choice."

"You mean, she may sleep with *anyone?*"

Pretty Sky laughed at him.

"No, not really. Certain relationships. Her husband's brother, maybe, if he has no wife. A young nephew . . . but no one in her *own* family line. That would be forbidden."

"Then it does not matter, who fathers her children?"

She could see that Bear Paws was bothered considerably by this entire conversation.

"It matters much, Bear Paws. She must *know* whose child she bears. That man must provide for the child, until it is grown. If she is with child by young Bent Arrow this month, *he* must provide, not her husband."

"But how . . . oh! That is why she must not be with her husband this month?"

"Of course. How could she tell which is the father?"

"*Aiee!* It is not so among *my* people."

Sky laughed at him, then realized that he considered this no laughing matter. He must be wondering . . .

"Bear Paws," she began seriously, "you are wondering about you and me?"

"Well, I . . ."

She snuggled against him, smiling provocatively.

"You have no brothers here?" she asked.

"No, of course not."

"No nephews?"

"You know that, Sky."

"Then," she whispered, "I must be content with you. But, I do not need anyone else. Come, let us walk."

The invitation to walk together was a special understanding between them. They had found romance difficult in the confines of the lodge, with others present, even in darkness. Therefore, they loved to slip away to a spot near the river, screened by willows and cottonwoods, and floored with soft meadow grass. They had spent many happy times in the privacy of this place. Pretty Sky had found that, when her husband seemed morose or worried, she could easily distract him, and make his world right again. The same was true for herself too, of course. Nearly any problem or misunderstanding that had come between them could be cured by a walk to their special place.

Other possible sources of misunderstanding were simple, however, compared to that which now faced them. Morning Star. It would be difficult. There were some even among her own people who were not comfortable with that ceremony. She doubted that Bear Paws would accept it as readily as he had accepted most of their ways. And she was very uncomfortable about avoiding his questions. Maybe she could postpone the inevitable explanations.

"That will be explained," she told him, "when someone has the vision."

Maybe no one will, she thought. *Maybe things will*

just get better. But she did not really believe it. Morning
Star had spoken to the priest, and His command must
be respected.

Maybe her husband's friend Red Hand would explain
to him. She knew that sometimes Bear Paws inquired of
his warrior-friend, in matters he did not understand.
Man-things. That would be good. Maybe Red Hand
could explain better than she, this thing of Morning
Star.

So, Pretty Sky busied herself with her children, and
with her tasks in the maintenance and management of
the lodge. She still hoped against hope that the vision
would not come, but there was a feeling of dread.
Somehow, she already felt the pressure of impending
events. There were dreams, fragmentary, discon-
nected, forgotten by morning. Except that the shadow
of the dream remained, hanging over her like a storm-
cloud, threatening and foreboding. There were partial
glimpses that kept recurring in the dream, glimpses of a
symbol or design, painted red . . . It looked familiar,
but for days she could not recall its significance. Then it
came to her. *Morning Star!* His sign.

It was of some comfort to recognize the sign. She did
not really see how it was of any direct threat to her or
her children. She had seen it all her life, the cross-
shaped symbol painted on the robe of the Morning Star
Priest. It seemed that . . . yes, on the sacred bundle of
Morning Star, too. It had been years since the bundle
was displayed publicly. The last time, of course, was
before Bear Paws joined the village. *Ah, how time flies,*
she thought.

Pretty Sky was quite uncertain why she should be
having glimpses of the symbol. Maybe it was part of the
vision they sought. But, only a man was to receive the
vision. She tried to dismiss it from her mind, but doubts

still troubled her. Somehow, impending events would affect her and her family. Well, so be it. If the vision came to one of the men as she supposed it would, everyone in the village would be affected.

That must be it. The power of the Morning Star spirit was everywhere, searching, looking for the right pathway . . . someone must be receptive. And in His search, she decided, Morning Star's spirit had encountered hers somewhere in the Dream-world. Having no use for her in His quest, He had passed on. It was a frightening thought, but in its own way, reassuring, now that she believed she had reasoned out what it meant.

She wondered if others, too, had felt the presence and seen the sign of Morning Star. Had Bear Paws' sleep been troubled? Or *could* it? Could her husband be the one chosen for the vision? Now that was certainly a chilling thought. No, surely not. Morning Star would not choose a complete outsider as the means to communicate His wishes. No, it would be someone else, some other man in the village, who would receive the vision. A young man, probably, because it would require great strength and daring. Yet, a warrior with some experience. Bent Arrow, perhaps? No, he had not yet experienced enough war parties. Her father, Lone Elk, was a respected leader, but his years were many. A younger man, maybe.

Besides, as she recalled, the choice of the visionary who would undertake the quest was usually a surprise. The few times in her life that Morning Star had spoken to her people, it was to someone not already prominent as a leader. This virtually eliminated all of the recognized leaders, priests, and holy men of the nation. It would be an unknown, a rising hero who would distinguish himself by his acceptance of this call. And, of course, the manner in which he carried out his responsibilities. There was a great deal of danger to the one selected. His duties would involve every bit of his time and effort, every thought and action, until after the ceremony was culminated in the spring. Even his own family must give him up until these duties were fulfilled.

Well, Pretty Sky decided, she would not worry about it. Her fragmentary dreams were merely a sign that the spirit of Morning Star had not abandoned her people. He was active and moving among them, searching for the man who would become His visionary. And when the time was ready, it would be revealed, and it would be good.

She had to admit, however, that she was glad that whoever was selected would *not* be her husband. It would not be pleasant, she thought, to lose him for such a long time, even for a noble calling like this one. It was hard to imagine, even, how Bear Paws would react to such a call. She smiled to herself at the thought of her husband becoming the custodian and protector of the Morning Star Maiden for a period of several moons.

No, it was better that he was an outsider, and not really eligible to be selected for the vision that would change the lives of them all.

3
»» »» »»

Many days' travel to the south, a young couple walked together in the cool of an autumn evening. They had spent many such intervals together, from the time they were small. In the Rabbit Society, when both boys and girls were learning the skills of the People, it was seen that these two, Calling Bird and Tall Bull, were drawn to each other.

It was a thing of the spirit, it seemed. There were private little jokes, at which no one laughed but these two. Sidelong glances, a shared thought that required no words to express. The two were well matched for skills, also. Both handled the throwing-clubs well, and made their first rabbit kills on the same day. When they were older, it was time to progress to the bow and arrow, the throwing-ax, and the lance. Their competition was friendly but fierce, and they rejoiced in each other's success, and were saddened by their failures.

The People were pleased by this friendship. This is

how it should be. It was assumed that when they came to maturity, Calling Bird and Tall Bull would set up their lodge together. These two were the shining example of what young people should be; attractive, capable, intelligent, and devoted to each other.

Others their age began to pair off and marry. There was no hurry for these two.

"When they are ready, they will tell us," a wise old woman observed.

Yet, as is so often the way of things, there were problems between these two, unknown and unseen by others. When Tall Bull became eligible for membership in a Warrior Society, it was assumed that now they would marry. Bull chose the Elk-dog Society, that of the horseman. But much to the surprise of all, Calling Bird also joined the Elk-dog Society. Not as a warrior, though that could have been a possibility. She chose the role of a Warrior Sister. This caused some uneasiness among the gossips of the Southern band.

"This allows them to be together, to perform the ceremonies together," said one.

"Yes, but it keeps them apart!" came the answer. "A Warrior Sister must take the vow of chastity."

"But only for now. When they are ready to marry, she can resign the vow."

The same discussion was carried on privately between the two principals in this situation.

"But why, Bird? You have proved yourself. Now, give up your sisterhood, and let us make our lodge together."

"It is mine to say," she insisted stubbornly. "My ancestor, Running Eagle, was a Warrior Sister. It is good to be like such a woman."

Now Tall Bull was even more concerned. The story of

that career was well known among the People. Running Eagle had gone on to become a warrior.

"But she became a warrior chief, Bird. Surely, you will not do that?"

She gave him a sidelong glance and tossed her head in a provocative gesture. It caused her shiny black hair, as bright as the wing of a crow, to spill across her shoulder in a most attractive way.

"I might," Calling Bird said tauntingly.

Tall Bull was even more frustrated, and turned away in anger. Unspoken, but hanging heavily between them was the fact that Running Eagle, in undertaking her warrior career, had continued her vows of chastity.

There were times when Calling Bird regretted the hurt that her teasing caused her friend. But, each time she decided to make amends, Tall Bull would do or say some small thing, some irritation that seemed to bring out the worst of mischief in her. Once more, she would taunt him.

So, it was not the happiest of times, as they walked together this evening. Both were silent for a long time. When they tried to talk, they always argued.

"It is good," Tall Bull finally broke the silence.

"What is good?" she asked.

"The evening . . . being with you."

She took his hand, and they walked along the stream, watching the colors change in the western sky.

"Sun Boy chooses his paints well tonight," noted Tall Bull. It was an old saying among the People, and he felt a little foolish at the obvious.

"That is true," agreed Calling Bird.

A coyote called on a distant ridge, and the hollow cry of *Kookooskoos*, the hunting owl, sounded from the trees along the river. They stopped for a moment as a sleek red fox crossed in front of them, pausing to turn

their way for a quick glance. The animal seemed un-
concerned, as if he knew that these two humans had no
designs on his life, at least for now.

"Bird," said Tall Bull carefully at last, "is it not time to
speak of the future?"

"Yours, or mine?" she asked quickly.

Instantly, she regretted her terse tone, and the hurt
that the thoughtless question implied.

"I had hoped both," he said glumly.

Somehow, his somber mood irritated the girl. As she
had become more non-committal about their relationship, her friend had seemed more withdrawn. Sometimes she longed for him to speak out in anger, to declare his love and sweep her away to the lodge they
would share. Instead, he became more hesitant.

Maybe this was the reason for her dreams. Those
bothered her some, making her feel disloyal to Tall
Bull. But maybe it was . . . *aiee,* how could she know?
Her dreams, though fragmentary and incomplete, always seemed to include a young man. She was never
able to see him clearly, but she knew that he was very
handsome. He seemed to glow, almost, with a shining
face . . . maybe that was why it was hard to look at.
His garments were of whitest buckskin, and trimmed
with red. There were unfamiliar symbols on the breast.

She had told no one of this dream. There was nothing
to tell, really. It was only that from time to time, she saw
this figure. He did nothing, said nothing, only looked at
her. Why, then, did she feel such a physical attraction to
this imaginary dream-figure, this spirit? It worried her,
because it was new to her experience. She could not
share the attraction that she felt with Tall Bull. There
was no one. Would another woman understand? Her
mother? No, she could not tell *her.* Her friends among
the other girls had established their own lodges now,

and were busy with their husbands and children. She wondered if she could approach the holy man, Red Horse, with such a thing. Could he explain its meaning?

Perhaps the most disturbing thing about her dream-hero was his strength, the dominance of his spirit. She could feel that, reaching out to her. There would be no time, she knew, that this man would be indecisive. She tried her best not to compare her impression of the stranger's cool confidence with the lack of decision on the part of her friend Tall Bull. She knew it was unfair to him, to compare his passive attitude to the strength of a dream-lover. If only he would take a firm stand, would tell her what he felt. Every exchange seemed to drive them further apart, which irritated her. This led to further cutting remarks, which drove them further . . . *aiee*, sometimes she felt that she was going mad! There must be some way to interrupt this cycle of hurt, misunderstanding, more hurt . . .

"What do you mean, both?" she snapped irritably, hating herself for it even as she spoke.

"Well, I thought we might speak of our lodge together."

They had spoken of this since they were children, that some day they would share a lodge. But now, somehow, it irritated her. What right did he have to assume such a thing? *Maybe I would share a lodge with someone else,* she thought. She started to say it aloud.

"Maybe I would . . ." She paused, confused.

How could she say such things to him, this best friend of her life? She could already see the hurt in his face.

"Maybe I would like to think on this, Bull," she said gently.

"As you say," he answered, obviously disappointed. "How long do you think this might take?"

"How do I know?" she snapped, and was sorry, even as she said it.

"Bird," he said seriously, "is there someone else?"

"No . . . no, of course not."

His question had startled her. She thought that he would know there was not. They had been so close, for so long, and he knew virtually all of her thoughts and feelings.

Except, of course, for this strange dream-thing lately. She had not been able to confide that. Now an odd thought struck her. *Was* there someone else? The dream-lover of her night-visions? She shook her head, puzzled and confused at these odd thoughts.

"I . . . I am sorry, Bull. I do not mean to be hurtful. It is only . . ." She stopped. *It is only what?* she thought. How could she explain? "I need a little time," she finished lamely.

Tall Bull sighed deeply.

"It is good," he said, though she knew it was not.

She could see the sadness and disappointment in his eyes. She longed to share her own doubts and troubles with him, so that they might comfort each other. But she could not, because he was a part of her doubts. She wanted him to be firm and sure, but at the same time resented him whenever he showed signs of being so.

She longed to be taken in his arms, to have him comfort her, as she would comfort him. But, she could not allow herself to do so, and was unsure why.

They turned back toward the camp, both feeling disappointed and unhappy.

4

>> >> >>

When the vision came to the village of the Pawnees, it was something of a relief. The waiting had become intolerable. At first, when the Morning Star Priest had announced the expected event, there was great excitement, an air of anticipation. Then, when nothing happened, the mood cooled.

Days passed, and there was no great difference in the repetitive existence. There was the daily routine of scant food, often of poor quality. More concern, on the part of the thoughtful members of the group, was for the winter months ahead. There would be times in the Moon of Long Nights and the Moon of Snows when there would be no hunting for days at a time. The carefully stored corn would be essential to survival. And even more important would be the preservation of part of that corn for next year's seed. Seven types in all, each kept separate and pure by keeping the fields the prescribed number of paces apart so that there would be no mixing. The purity of the four wind-directional corns, especially, must be preserved. The four colors; white, yellow, blue, and red, the colors that formed the basis for the ceremonials, must be unquestionably pure. Two perfect ears in the medicine-bundle of each wind, ceremonially changed each season. Such concerns were the responsibility of the priests, but any thoughtful person was concerned that these things must be carried out.

So, for a matter of perhaps half a moon, there was probably more concern for the coming winter than for the expected Morning Star vision. When it came, it was almost an anticlimax.

The one selected was an odd choice. Hunts-Well had never really distinguished himself at anything. He was one of those who always seem to be at the wrong place at the wrong time, missing the excitement and the glory of any meaningful event. Even his name had been bestowed almost as a joke, at about the time he came to manhood. His life seemed to be so colorless that there was really no distinguishing feature about it, by which he could be known.

Finally, in the informal circle of warrior-hunters who were discussing the upcoming young men, one had made an observation.

"At least, he *hunts* well."

There had been a chuckle around the circle. There was a subtle difference between hunting *well* and hunting *successfully,* and this was the basis for the joke. It was told and retold in the band. It might have been forgotten, except that a number of the young men had gone out on a short hunt for deer a day or two later. This particular individual, though he had evaluated the wind, the light, and the movements of the animals, was unsuccessful. Some stray puff of breeze carrying human scent, perhaps . . . at any rate, his bow had not launched a single arrow that day, while his companions boasted three kills. Just one of those things.

"Even though he hunted well," related one of the other youths, unaware of the quiet joke being told among the older men.

And the name stuck, as a nickname spoken in jest sometimes will.

Hunts-Well had grown to maturity and married a not-very-attractive woman of one of the less distinguished families of the band. They had produced three rather ordinary children. Altogether, he would have been considered a very unlikely candidate for the vision that would save the village.

He was middle-aged now, secretly disappointed that he had never managed to accomplish anything worthy of recounting around the story fires. His children were grown, and they in turn were rather undistinguished. So even Hunts-Well was astonished when the vision came.

He had been sleeping poorly for several nights. He had attributed it to the changing season. Everyone was a bit restless at this time of year. The temperature was unpredictable, hot days and cool nights. The southward migration of waterfowl was in progress, and there was always restless excitement in the cry of the long lines of geese in the night sky.

On the night that the vision came, he had arisen and gone outside the lodge to relieve his bladder. The stars were bright, and the air crisp and cool. He was glad to get back inside and seek the comfort of his robes and his wife's warm body beside him. But she turned knees and elbows toward him, so he wrapped in the robe instead. Soon that became too warm, and he tossed it aside restlessly.

Finally, when he drifted off to sleep, it was nearly dawn. But almost immediately he began to dream. There was a white light, one that hurt his eyes, shining through the trees outside his own village. He walked toward it, puzzled, yet not afraid. A stranger stood there, and the light seemed to come from the stranger, or maybe from behind him. The man was a handsome young warrior, dressed in a ceremonial tunic and leggings of white buckskin, decorated with red symbols.

Hunts-Well tried to speak, but words would not come. He shakily tried hand-signs.

"How are you called?"

"I am Morning Star," the stranger said, in a deep clear voice that seemed to fill the clearing. "Your people have forgotten me!"

"No, no," Hunts-Well started to protest, but the shining visitor silenced him with the wave of a hand.

"Be still and listen! Here is what you must do. I require a wife, and you are to find her and bring her to me."

"But I . . ."

"Silence! You will travel to the southwest, where she waits."

"How can I do this?" blurted Hunts-Well. "Why *me?*"

"Because you are *chosen!*" thundered the answer. "Go to my priest, and tell him what I have said!"

The vision began to fade, and in a few heartbeats, Hunts-Well could see the trees on the other side of the clearing *through* the torso of the young man.

"Wait!" he cried. "How . . ."

Just then he awoke, in his own robes, wet with sweat. The first dim light of dawn was peeping through the doorway, around the skin that hung as a curtain. The others in the lodge were not yet awake.

Still shaken by his dream, he rose and stumbled outside. Had it been real? Morning Star . . . he whirled and looked to the east, but there was a misty appearance to the gray-yellow of the dawn. He could not be sure, even, whether one of the stars he saw *was* the Star of Morning. There was too much fog.

He was frightened, and fought down the urge to run wildly into the prairie. Breathing heavily, he walked a little way and leaned against a tree. His face was numb, and his hands and feet felt wooden and useless. Was he *dying?* Could he tell anyone about this experience, if indeed he did not die? *Wait,* he thought. *I must think about this calmly.*

He forced himself to slow his breathing, and in a little while he began to feel better. Still, the significance of his dream had not quite come through to him. Morning Star . . . in his wildest imaginings, Hunts-Well had never considered that the one selected for the vision might be himself. He was a nobody. He knew that there were those who laughed at him behind his back. Most people, however, did not even bother to do that. They merely ignored him, looked right through him sometimes, as a non-person, a nobody. He would have thought that the one selected would be one of the young sub-chiefs, a real leader. Maybe he had been reached by mistake. Maybe Morning Star had come, looking for some other man, and Hunts-Well had merely happened to get up to empty his bladder at the wrong time. That would be more likely.

But no . . . he had gone *back* to the lodge, before the vision came! Yet, how could he ever convince anyone that *he* was the one?

The words of Morning Star came back to him, ringing clear: *Go to my priest, and tell him what I have said!*

Numbly, Hunts-Well stumbled back among the lodges toward the dwelling of the Morning Star Priest.

People were beginning to emerge sleepily from their lodges, stretching and yawning. Some nodded or spoke to him, but he did not answer. Straight ahead he plodded, shuffling through the dust as it lay still damp in the morning dew. He stopped at the lodge he sought and knocked on the door post.

"Uncle," he called out, "I must speak with you!"

There was stirring inside, and old Hawk's Tail looked out, still rubbing the sleep from his eyes.

"Yes . . . what is it?"

"Morning Star has spoken to me."

A look of incredibility came over the face of the holy man.

"*You?*" he asked.

Then he seemed to compose himself.

"Come inside," he invited more calmly. "You must tell me all you have seen and heard."

First, the priest seated his guest and gave him a few bites of a ceremonial corn cake and a sip of water. Then, when Hunts-Well had finished, he began the interrogation. All others had been banished from the lodge.

"Now, tell me . . ."

"I had been up to go outside, Uncle . . ."

"Yes, yes, but the vision! Go on!"

"Yes. It was in a dream."

The priest nodded.

"I saw this stranger, bright with light, who said that he was Morning Star. He said that I was to find and bring his wife. Uncle, I know nothing of such things. I am afraid."

"No, do not be afraid," soothed the priest. "What else did he tell you?"

"I must go southwest. His wife is there."

"And that is all?"

"Yes . . . I was to come to you."

"It is good," said the priest. "Now, we will both eat a little, and then go outside to make the announcement."

"But, I do not understand. What are my duties?"

"We will speak of that, later. It will be told to you."

"Another vision?"

"Maybe. But probably not. You will learn through me."

"Where . . . ?"

"Where will you go? That will be given you. You will choose warriors to go with you. But come, now. Let us eat the sacred meal, and then we will go out to meet the dawn and tell the people."

The sun was rising when the two men stepped from the lodge to greet the gathering crowd. It had been apparent that something important was underway, when the priest's family was sent from the lodge. Hawk's Tail waited a moment for quiet, and then spoke.

"Morning Star has spoken to us," he announced. There was a brief murmur of excitement, and he waited again for quiet, as well as for effect. "Our brother, Hunts-Well, has been chosen," he announced. "He will lead the search party for the bride. They will leave, four days from now."

Hunts-Well drew himself up with pride. Never again would people make jokes about him. Now he had become a most important man, and would be one of those spoken to with respect. It felt good, this matter of becoming one of the chosen. In years to come, he would be pointed out to visitors. Not as a joke, a failure, a nonperson. No, this was a great day in his life.

"That is Hunts-Well," people would say. "He was chosen as Wolf-man for Morning Star."

5

>> >> >>

Pretty Sky and Bear Paws joined the crowd, as excitement mounted.

"Hunts-Well?" people asked each other incredulously.

"So says Hawk's Tail. The vision came in the late-night time, only this morning."

"Well, if Morning Star's priest says so . . . ."

"What happens now?" Bear Paws asked his wife.

"I cannot remember, Bear. It has been a long time. I was quite young, you know."

He nodded, too preoccupied with the excitement to notice her attempt at a joke about her age when they had met.

"Hawk's Tail will tell us, maybe," she finished.

Now the Morning Star Priest was holding up both hands for silence. The crowd quieted.

"All of you know," began Hawk's Tail, "that one of our brothers has been chosen to receive the vision we have sought. Morning Star came to him this very morning."

The old man paused for effect, a master at creating the suspense necessary to sustain the excitement. The crowd remained silent, waiting.

"I have heard his dream-vision," he went on, "and I am made to think that Hunts-Well is truly the chosen one."

Now an excited murmur rippled through the crowd, and quickly quieted. Hawk's Tail looked slowly around the area, his dignity impressive, his authority unquestioned. He turned to face the east, and raised his arms again.

"O, Morning Star, we thank you for this sign that you have given to our brother. May he be given the help that he needs to fulfill his quest."

"What quest, Sky?" her husband whispered.

"Ssh—he will tell us, I think."

The Morning Star Priest continued.

"Our brother will pray and fast for four days, now," he went on. "During that time he will choose the warriors who will go with him. They will go to the south."

"Maybe I could be of help to him," Bear Paws whispered. "That is the territory of my people."

Sky looked at him, startled, but quickly recovered her composure.

"No, I think not," she said. "This is a holy quest, and you are still an outsider."

He nodded in understanding. The thought had crossed his mind that he might be able to contact his parents, visit them, or at least send a message, through someone in the Northern band. But, he could understand that this was a holy quest. His background and his spiritual training simply made him unacceptable as a volunteer. In most respects, Bear Paws was accepted completely by his wife's people. But this was a thing of the spirit. This was similar to a situation among his own people; only certain hunters were authorized to obtain the special buffalo to be used for the annual Sun Dance. He dismissed the thought that he had had, that of acting as a guide for whatever quest was beginning.

"How far south will they go?" he asked.

Pretty Sky shrugged.

"I do not know, Bear. They will probably not tell us. Maybe Hunts-Well does not even know. His vision may have given only a direction, not a place."

That, too, was understandable. A quest of any sort would often begin quite vaguely, and more details be revealed along the way.

The crowd began to break up now, going their separate ways. Hunts-Well turned away, accompanied by the holy man. He would begin his fast immediately, as well as his songs and prayers, under the direction of the Morning Star Priest.

Four warriors were selected to form the base of the quest party. It was unclear to Bear Paws whether the choices were made by Hawk's Tail, the holy man, or by the visionary, Hunts-Well. Maybe both. The announcements were made publicly and with much ceremony, and the chosen warriors were given much honor.

The priest then requested any who would volunteer, as a sort of honor guard for those designated. Immediately, there were many who would go. In the excitement of the moment, Bear Paws again felt that he should volunteer. It was easy to be caught up in the spirit of this thing. In a way it was much like the feeling that he had always had for the Sun Dance festival among his own people. There was a religious fervor, a pleasant tension, and a feeling that good things were to happen. He realized, of course, that as an outsider, he could not volunteer for this mission. He must be one of those to stay behind, to protect the village, and do what little hunting might be possible, until the return of the quest party.

As it happened, there were many volunteers. So many, in fact, that Hawk's Tail was forced to limit participation.

"It is enough!" he announced. "So many cannot move without being obvious. This must not look like a war party."

Bear Paws was puzzled at such a remark. The implication was strong, that the true purpose of the quest must be concealed from those whose territory they would enter. Again, Pretty Sky was quite vague when he inquired about it.

"Well, it is not a war party," she answered. "It should not look like one."

"Then what is it? What will they do? What do they seek?"

"I do not know, Bear Paws. It is a command of Morning Star. You would not understand, anyway. Your people do not know Morning Star."

It was like a slap across the face. He turned, angry and frustrated, and stalked away. There was an unfairness here, a hint that he could not understand because his people were inferior. In addition, it was a personal offense, this high-handed dismissal by his wife. It was as if something had come between them, destroying much of what they had shared in closeness and understanding.

He left the village and climbed the slight slope to a knoll where he sometimes went to think and meditate, alone from the busy life below. He had seldom come here angry. By nature he was not combative, but easy-going and tolerant. This had helped him greatly in his attempts to adapt to the completely different ways of his wife's people. In addition, Pretty Sky had always been helpful, explaining and encouraging.

It was doubly frustrating, then, to have her unwilling to explain this Morning Star custom. She had also talked down to him, as if he were a child. She had not even done that when he had doubts about their friend Bent Arrow and his brother's wife. She had explained their sexual customs. Strange customs, by the standards of the People, but *their* customs. If Bear Paws lived with his wife's people, it seemed that he should follow their customs as well as he could. He had tried to do so, and they had seemed to approve his efforts. Even his wife's mother, Kills-Three, had finally come to treat him well. He never had learned, however, how the woman had earned such a name. He was not sure he wanted to know.

But this thing of Morning Star . . . he could not understand. Pretty Sky shrugged off his questions with vague answers that told him nothing. He was certain from her attitude that she knew much more than she was telling him. That hurt was bad enough, but to belittle him and the spiritual understanding of his people was completely unfair.

Worst of all, their marriage had lost something. Whatever the mystery of this vision by Hunts-Well, and its subsequent quest, there was something ominous about it. Otherwise, Sky would not hesitate to share it with him. That, in turn, had driven an obstacle between them. Bear Paws was uncertain about the threat that seemed to hang over him. It was there, without question, a heaviness of the heart that was undeniable. But what was it, this thing he had begun to dread? What dark unspoken threat was connected to the excitement of the quest party's mission? And he was completely unable to decide whether that was the reason for his heavy heart. Maybe it was simply that it seemed to be destroying his marriage. Maybe, both.

Whatever the reason, he and Pretty Sky had never seemed farther apart. Even in his early days as a prisoner of these Horn People, he had always felt that she was trying to help him. Now, that was gone. Pretty Sky was secretive, deceptive, and was ready to belittle him and his people because of their different spirit-ways.

Day by day, they went about their routine. To most observers, there was probably nothing amiss. But to Bear Paws, there was something dreadfully wrong. He and Pretty Sky were growing farther apart. Even the shared joy in their children did not quite overcome the heavy ache in his heart. Possibly, even, it was worse, the pretending that all was well, yet knowing otherwise.

The quest party had been gone for half a moon, now. Bear Paws had hoped that as things settled back to normal, he and Sky might recover what they had lost. It was not so. If anything, the situation was becoming worse. There was no way to guess when the party might return, and he hesitated to bring up the subject with Sky again. She was withdrawn and morose, and spoke to him only when necessary.

He must talk to someone . . . *Red Hand!* Ah, yes! Bear Paws wondered why he had not thought of it before. He felt that he could not discuss the problems with his marriage, but somehow, that was intertwined with this Morning Star thing. If he could ask his friend of that, maybe he could find what there was about it that was pulling Pretty Sky away from him.

He was glad that Red Hand had not gone with Hunts-Well. He would have been a good man for such a quest, whatever it was. But his skills also made Red Hand a good man to stay behind to protect and hunt for the village. This, too, created a kinship and understanding among those who remained at home. *It is good!* Bear Paws thought to himself. He would seek out Red Hand to talk, this very day.

6

>> >> >>

"**H**o, my friend, let us hunt! I am tired of doing nothing."

Red Hand looked up from where he sat, smoking quietly in the autumn sunlight.

"Ho, Bear Paws! Sit, let us share a pipe and talk of this, first."

Red Hand had just lighted his pipe, and it was burning, slowly and well. One does not interrupt such a pleasant interlude without some consideration.

Bear Paws sat down, and took a couple of puffs from the pipe that his friend hospitably offered. The fragrant bluish smoke hung for a moment in the still air, and then dissipated into nothing, leaving behind only its warm fragrance.

"That is good," noted Bear Paws, returning the pipe. "What is it?"

Red Hand smiled.

"A mixture . . . the trader who was here told me of

it. Sumac, a few cedar berries. Tobacco, of course. The trader called it *kinnikinik.* He learned of it from some tribe he visited. They used red willow sometimes, too, he said."

Bear Paws nodded. "My people use the sumac. A little cedar, sometimes. Red willow?"

"Yes. Maybe we should try it."

Bear Paws nodded again, but he was thinking of other things.

"Shall we look for antelope today?" Actually, he was not really concerned with antelope, either, except incidently. It would be good to find meat, too, of course, but his primary aim was to take his friend aside to ask about the mystery and excitement that seemed to surround the Morning Star vision.

"Maybe to the north," suggested Red Hand. "Shall we ask Badger to go?"

"No," Bear Paws answered quickly. "Two are enough. The antelope have been hunted hard. More hunters will drive them off."

The other nodded, and offered the pipe again. They finished the pipeful, making small talk about the weather. Red Hand rose.

"Let us go," he suggested. "The sun grows higher."

The two men selected their horses, and adjusted saddle pads and bridle thongs. Swinging up, they rode northward, away from the river and its accompanying trees. It was always good to Bear Paws, to ride out into open prairie again. It was not quite like the prairie of his people, the sacred Tallgrass Hills, but at least it was open country. A rider could see horizons a day's journey away. There were times when the trapped feeling of living in a permanent lodge of mud and logs almost overcame him. The cure was a ride or a hunt in open prairie, a chance to see far expanses, to regain the feel of man's place in the world. He always felt better after a hunt of this sort, successful or not. This setting, too, seemed appropriate for a talk about things of the spirit.

They rode and hunted for some time, searching possible areas that might be attractive to the far-ranging antelope. None were seen.

"Let us go to that rise, and look from there." Red Hand pointed to a low ridge.

They turned in that direction, climbed the slope, and dismounted at the summit. For a little while, they observed in all directions, while the horses began to graze on the short grass.

"I see nothing," said Red Hand. "You?"

"Nothing . . . let us wait a little."

They sat without talking for a time, and finally Bear Paws ventured to begin the conversation.

"Red Hand, you have been good to tell me of the customs of your people."

"It is nothing. I tried to kill you once, too."

Both laughed. It was a standing joke between them.

"True," agreed Bear Paws, "but that was when I was the enemy. Or, you thought so."

"You were *with* the enemy."

"Yes, yes, but let me go on."

Red Hand nodded agreeably.

"Now there are many things about your people that I do not understand," Bear Paws went on.

"Of course. You have been with us only four . . . five winters?"

"Yes. Tell me of the Morning Star quest, which Hunts-Well leads."

"What do you wish to know?"

"Well, where do they go, what is their purpose?"

"Oh. They seek a wife for Morning Star."

"Yes, someone said that."

"Then, you know."

"No! Remember, I am an outsider, Red Hand. Tell me . . ."

"Well, you know of our Creation Story?"

"Yes. Part of it, anyway. It is much more involved than ours."

"Yes. Then you know that Evening Star is Morning Star's woman?"

"Yes," answered Bear Paws.

"Well, it was not always so. In the beginning *Tirawa,* the Great Spirit, ordered them to marry, but Evening Star did not wish to do so. So, she stationed fierce animals in all four directions: a wolf, a bear, a cougar, I do not remember. Ah, Bear, I am no storyteller."

"Go on."

"Well, Evening Star killed them all, and approached her bed. Even then, she tried to stop him. There were rattlesnakes in her bed."

"Aiee!" laughed Bear Paws. "He must have wanted her badly!"

"He had no choice. *Tirawa* had decreed it. Anyway, they finally got together, and had a child, a girl, who was the first human being. That is why Evening Star is called sometimes 'Mother of Earth.' She and Morning Star still do not get along well. They move together and then apart again, through the seasons."

"I see. They have had other children, then?"

"No! First Man was born from a marriage of Sun and Moon. That is how humans came to be."

"But what has all this to do . . . ?"

"You are too impatient, Bear Paws. I am trying to tell you. Morning Star gave his daughter to become the first woman. He expects to be repaid."

"Repaid?"

"Yes. He and his wife, Evening Star, still argue and

fight sometimes, and his bed is lonely. So, he seeks a
new, younger wife to warm his bed from time to time.
He gives instructions in a vision, where to find her."

"And, Hunts-Well has had this vision?"

"Yes. They have gone to find the bride."

Bear Paws was completely confused.

"They find a *star* for him?"

"No, no! A girl. A human. She must be a virgin. That is
what he gave Earth, and he must be repaid with the
same, a human virgin."

Bear Paws was startled, but tried to maintain his composure.

"How is this done?" he asked.

"Well, the girl will be shown to them. They will per-
suade her to come back here, where she is a person of
great honor. She has the finest of food, eaten from special bowls. Fine dresses. There are women to fix her
hair, one man, the Wolf-man, who stays with her all the
time to protect her and see that she remains pure. That
is Hunts-Well, who is directed by the vision."

"How long does this go on?"

"Until time for the ceremony. Hawk's Tail is told
when. In the spring, sometime."

"He has a vision?"

"No. He watches for Morning Star. The appearance
must be just right. I have heard that Morning Star turns
red to signal the ceremony."

"Then what happens?"

"I do not know it all, Bear Paws. There are ceremonies, in a lodge. Several of the priests take part. A sacred
star fire, of poles made of different woods. It must burn
for four days and nights. There are ceremonies each
day, changes of costume for the priests and the bride.
The Morning Star Priest is the leader."

"You have seen this, Red Hand?"

"No, not inside the lodge. There is a public ceremony on the fifth morning. I have seen that, but it has been a few years. Morning Star does not require a woman every year. Only when the corn begins to grow poorly. That is how the priest knows Morning Star must be lonely."

"And this ceremony?"

"It is in early morning, just before dawn, when Morning Star is seen well. It is carried out as he rises. The priests prepare a marriage bed, of soft down-feathers, with a scaffold above. The bride climbs up the scaffold . . . like a ladder . . . to join her husband."

Bear Paws had long since become confused. Apparently this virgin bride was to be from a tribe other than this. She was to be "persuaded" to accept this office, and brought back to the Horn People to live in honor. Red Hand had not specified how it could be that a young woman would consent to this. And climbing a ladder to join her husband, Morning Star . . . ? There were more questions here than he had had before. Something was missing in the story, or in his understanding of it.

"I do not understand this at all, my friend," he said. "This is much different than my people."

"Of course. All nations have different customs. That is why we are talking."

Bear Paws thought a moment. From his childhood came the memory of words of caution to young girls. *Be careful. Do not go far from the camp. You will be stolen!* Was this the same thing? Traditionally, there were some of the neighboring tribes who had raided the People for wives. *Our women are prettier than theirs* was a phrase he had heard all his life. It was partially true. The women of the People were tall, long-legged, and well-formed, very desirable as wives. The practice of wife-stealing had diminished in later years. Especially, it was said, since the alliance with the Head Splitters a generation or two ago. Head Splitters had been one of the worst raiding groups. Now, any intermarriage was in friendship. No, this was something else entirely, it appeared.

But what? There were still more questions than answers, and this bothered him.

"Red Hand," he asked, "*how* does the bride join Morning Star? She cannot climb to the stars on her ladder."

"Of course not. There is only one way to reach the stars . . . to become one of them. She must die and cross over."

A cold hand gripped the heart of Bear Paws. He had finally guessed, but did not really want to hear.

"How . . . ?" he asked softly.

"With the Sacred Arrow. When the bride is aligned with Morning Star as he rises, the priest shoots her, and her marriage to Morning Star is complete."

"She is *killed?*"

"Of course. How else could she join her husband?"

Bear Paws thought that he could never quite feel the same about Red Hand. Or, perhaps, about any of his wife's people. Could he even continue to live with them?

"Now you know the worst," Red Hand was saying. "But, you must also know this, my friend. There are many who believe this to be an evil thing. They are quiet because of the power of the Morning Star Priest. There is little that can be done."

7
>> >> >>

Hunts-Well and one of his party lay at full length on the flat-topped hill observing the encampment below. A hundred or more large skin lodges were scattered across the level floor of the valley. Beyond, a horse herd grazed under the supervision of a few of the young men.

"Is this the place we seek?" asked No-Tail-Squirrel.

"I am made to think so," said Hunts-Well.

"These are the Elk-dog People?"

"Yes, so we were told by the Growers."

Hunts-Well could not have said how he knew this to be their goal. He still marveled at how the entire sequence of events was happening to him. They had traveled long days to reach this place, and he did not know why or how, but this was the place. Here lived the Morning Star Princess, who would accompany them back to the Platte.

"What shall we do now?" asked his companion.

"We will go in," stated Hunts-Well. "Not all of us. That would attract too much attention. Only a few. Come."

Yes, that would be the plan. They wriggled backward, away from the rim of the hill, until they were out of sight of the camp. Then they rose.

"Come," he said again, leading the way along a dim game trail toward the ravine where the others waited with the horses.

"Four of us will go in," he told them. It was odd, the feeling of power that he now had, as leader of this party. What a difference it had made, the vision. Now he was respected, envied. The feeling was good, especially to one who had never before been a leader of anything.

"You others wait here," Hunts-Well continued. "We will circle and come into their camp from the southwest, so it looks like we are returning home."

The others nodded in understanding.

"We will be back tomorrow," he assured them.

"What if you are not?" asked Beaver Tail.

Hunts-Well looked at the questioner with a withering stare.

"We will return tomorrow, Beaver. I have spoken."

Now that the prestige and authority were his, he would not tolerate any question or challenge.

"Of course," mumbled the embarrassed Beaver Tail. No one else spoke.

Hunts-Well designated those who would accompany him: No-Tail-Squirrel, Plenty-Snows, and Mountain. They mounted their horses to begin the circuitous route around the encampment of the Elk-dog People below. It would take until late afternoon. They must seek out valleys and ravines, to remain out of sight of the "wolves" or scouts who would be constantly circling to watch for intruders.

"No fires," Hunts-Well cautioned as he turned his horse away.

The others nodded. The four horsemen rode up the valley, heading for a notch in the hills that formed a ridge to the west. It was important, Hunts-Well knew, that they give every appearance of having traveled a long way. From Santa Fe, perhaps. Yes, that would be a good story. They were returning from a trading expedition to the southwest, where they sought metal knives and arrow points. But how, then, could they explain that they carried no such items? He thought about that a little while.

Maybe . . . yes, they could claim to be only an exploring party, testing to see whether the trade would be reasonable. An item or two . . .

"Snows," he asked, "you have your new knife?"

"Yes. What . . . ?"

"Nothing. It is good. We will tell them you just traded for it in Santa Fe. Mountain's fire-striker, too. Yes, that is good. We have been to see if the trade would be good in Santa Fe."

They rode a while longer, and another thought struck him. *Ah, of course!* he told himself.

"Come," he told his companions. "Let us run the horses a while. They must appear to have come a long distance."

He kicked his horse into a lope.

It was nearly evening when the four travelers rode their tired horses into the camp. Both mounts and riders were covered with trail dust, and dried sweat crusted along the necks and flanks of the animals. The four were flanked by two of the wolves who had watched them come in across the prairie. The western sky was ablaze with the gold and orange of the autumn sunset.

"Greetings!" Hunts-Well signed to the dignified man who emerged from one of the lodges. This must be the leader of this band. The scouts had brought the visitors to pay the customary respects to their chief. The man raised a right hand in the answering greeting, and then signed a question.

"How are you called?"

"I am Hunts-Well, of the Pawnee. You call us Horn People."

The chief nodded. This was apparent from the horn-shaped hair-locks on the heads of the riders.

"We have traveled far," Hunts-Well continued. "We would camp with you tonight, if it pleases you."

The chief nodded graciously.

"It is good. Where have you traveled?"

"Southwest," Hunts-Well gestured.

"Hunting?"

"No, trading." Now would be the critical moment. Their story must be believable. It was apparent that they were too far from home for a hunt, and that they carried no trade goods.

"Trading?"

"Yes. We have been to the southwest. A place called Santa Fe. You know it?"

The chief nodded. "Our people have traded there." His look was cautious, a little suspicious, maybe.

"But we never have," admitted Hunts-Well. "We only went there to see if it could be done. We took a few skins . . . beaver, fox. What was easy to carry."

He drew his knife, a shiny new steel sheath-knife, one of his most prized possessions.

"I traded for this, and Mountain, there, for the metal fire-striker he carries. We go again, next season."

The chief nodded.

"It is good. Stay with us tonight, then. We will eat, smoke, light the story fires."

"It is good."

"Our young men will show you a good place to camp," the chief continued. "Upstream, there."

Hunts-Well signed his thanks and turned away, pleased. It was going well. There appeared to be no suspicion at all, and their story of an exploratory trip to investigate the possibility of trade seemed to be well accepted.

Now, he must be looking carefully for the girl he sought, yet not be too obvious about it. It would be understandable that men who had been traveling, and away from their wives, might look admiringly at a woman. But, they must not overdo it. Hunts-Well was uncertain about the customs of these people. Some of the hunting tribes had strange ways. He had heard, even, that among some, a woman would bed only with her husband. He had cautioned the others. This was certainly not the time to offend their hosts. That was merely good sense anyway, but with the added importance of their mission, they must be even more careful.

A woman walked by, and Hunts-Well eyed her appreciatively. *Ah, these women are good to look upon,* he thought. Tall, long-legged, proud of bearing, and well-formed. But he must not be distracted. A *young* woman . . . she could be as young as twelve or thirteen summers, Hawk's Tail had told him. The important thing was her purity. She must be a maiden to please Morning Star, one who had never been with a man. *That one?* No, not yet in the flower of womanhood . . . another. *Yes, that might be the one.* But no . . . no sooner had he begun to consider than a small child toddled to the woman and reached to be picked up. He moved on.

They established their camp, and settled in, lighting their fire to establish their presence. As twilight deepened, a young man came to invite the visitors to come to the center of the camp.

"Our chief invites you to smoke with him," the youth signed.

Good. This would be the preliminary to the storytelling, and would bring nearly everyone together. These people would naturally be curious about strangers, and would come to see. That, in turn, would allow the visitors to look over the eligible maidens. Hunts-Well was still puzzled as to how he would identify the Bride, but Hawk's Tail had assured him that it would be no problem.

"She will be revealed to you," the priest had said.

He still wondered *how,* still studied each woman who passed, and hoped that his ogling was not too obvious.

Then, as they smoked with the chief and a circle of men who appeared to have special leadership status, it happened. They were still making small talk in handsigns, talk of weather and game and the season. The more interesting part of the evening was yet to come, but people were already gathering, to assure themselves of good places around the story fire. As curious people walked past, pausing to look at the strangers, Hunts-Well glanced up, startled. He was looking into a pair of large dark eyes, like pools of deep water. These eyes were set in a face that was strikingly beautiful. As his eyes swept downward over the girl's body, he hoped that his thoughts were not too obvious. She was tall, well-formed, yet willowy and supple in the way she moved.

This is the one, he thought. But no, a young man stood with her . . . her husband? If so, she would be useless for Morning Star's purpose. Hunts-Well studied the pair a moment longer. The girl smiled, a pleasant sunny smile. Her companion seemed disgruntled, jealous, perhaps.

No! Hunts-Well thought triumphantly. *They do not belong to each other!* He sensed some sort of friction between them, and intense interest on the part of the girl. Also, he noted with pleasure, she was an ideal candidate for Morning Star. There was a look of pride about her, a sense of confidence in her stately bearing. He nodded politely, the girl returned his nod, and the two moved on to find a seat.

It was difficult to conceal his elation, he was so sure of this as the maiden Morning Star had selected. All through the evening, he glanced at her from time to time. Occasionally she would catch his eye and smile back. It was a thrilling thing, exciting beyond belief. During his years of courting, he had never had such an experience. A beautiful young woman, smiling at him, a stranger, with interest and excitement apparent in the firelight reflected from her eyes. He did not delude himself. He knew that her interest was not in Hunts-Well, a middle-aged nobody. The fire in her eyes was for what he represented, for *Morning Star.*

Hunts-Well, in turn, was excited, far beyond any physical attraction he might have had for this young woman. He could feel the power, the attraction that he was exerting on this desirable maiden, as a representative of the deity, a visionary for Morning Star.

8

>> >> >>

It was probably the most heated argument that the two had ever had. How silly of Tall Bull, she thought, to be jealous of these travelers. They would be gone today, tomorrow at the latest. True, they were strange men, with their shaven heads and their remaining hair shaped into a top-knot that resembled a horn growing out of the skull. Calling Bird had been fascinated by them at the story fire last night. Tall Bull had obviously misunderstood her interest, and had become irritated at her.

That point, she now realized, was when she should have backed away. But he had been so amusing, and it was so much fun to tease him. Besides, it was ridiculous for him to behave so. She had felt at first that at any moment he would dissolve into shared laughter, as they had done so many times before.

But it did not happen, and they parted when the stories were over, both angry and resentful. She had not slept well, and she knew that Tall Bull probably had not either. At daybreak, she slipped quietly out of the lodge and down to the stream to wash her face and comb her hair. Then she walked, slowly, lost in thought.

Why had the one Horn-man looked at her so strangely? She was accustomed to admiring glances from men. She was aware of her beauty, though not vain about it. She had always thought her nose a trifle too large, maybe . . . her cheekbones too sharp. But one is never entirely pleased with one's own appearance. Other women considered her most attractive. The eyes of men had followed her since the bloom of her womanhood had first begun to bud.

So, it was not remarkable that the visitors had looked at her with admiration. That, she had to admit, was pleasing. She was proud to attract such glances, as any woman should be. She had smiled appreciatively, knowing that nothing would come of it. Except, of course, the little jealousy of Tall Bull. That, of course, was acceptable, even amusing.

Somewhere along the way, however, things had gotten out of hand. Calling Bird was still puzzled about that. What had happened, and when? Tall Bull had become more jealous and irritable, and she had teased him. A little too much, maybe. She regretted that, now. She had not intended to make him so angry. When she saw him she would try to mend that error.

Still, all of this did not explain the other . . . the way the one man had watched her. It was different. His spirit reached out, seeking her, powerfully and demanding; yet, in a strange way. It was not that he wanted her in a physical way. She was familiar with *that* look, too. This was curiously different. It was an admiring stare, yet . . . *aiee,* it was confusing. And the strange mark on his forehead in red paint. She had seen that somewhere before. It made her a little nervous, but she kept glancing back to see if he still watched her. A few times their eyes met, and she had smiled nervously. What else could she do? The man's expression had not changed.

Probably she would have left the story fire early and gone home, if it had not been for Tall Bull and his amusing jealousy. She had never seen that side of him before, and it was interesting to play with. Yes, she had overdone it, and regretted her actions.

She was pleased, then, when she saw a familiar figure ahead of her.

"Tall Bull!" she called. Now everything would be right.

Her friend turned and came toward her. She could see by his grim expression that he was still hurting.

"Bull," she began gently, "my heart is heavy over last night."

"As it should be!" he snapped.

She felt the anger rise within her, and her wish for reconciliation faded.

"You have no right to talk to me like that!" she retorted.

"I have every right! You flirted shamelessly."

"I did not! I smiled politely."

"At a man as old as your father. Bird, it is not good. I saw how this man looked at you."

"And why should a man not look at me?" she demanded. "I have not been spoken for."

"But I . . ."

"I do not belong to you, Bull. Remember, I am a Warrior Sister. I may even decide to become a warrior, and continue my chastity vows."

That was a cruel thrust, and she knew it, but she was angry.

Tall Bull was trying to regain his calm. He took a deep breath or two, and when he finally spoke, his voice trembled.

"Calling Bird, I would not try to tell you what to do. You know that. But be careful. Something is not right about these men. Especially the older one, with the mark on his forehead."

She was startled. So Tall Bull had felt it, too! A strange thing for him to notice, yet not really. She longed to pour forth her thoughts and confusion, but she was still too angry. She tried to control it, choke it down.

"No matter," she said stiffly. "They will soon be gone."

"None too soon. Will you avoid them?" He paused, then continued. "I do not mean to tell you what to do, Bird. It is only that I fear for you. You should not come out of camp alone."

"Nonsense! I can take care of myself!" She was becoming irritated again.

"Normally, yes! But we do not know what these men want. That one with the little four-cornered star on his forehead . . . he does not want you as a man wants a woman. There is something else."

Again, she was startled. There *was* something, a thing so powerful that Tall Bull was feeling it, too. But how could it be described?

"Bull," she said seriously, "I feel this, too. I do not know what. But do not worry. I need to think about it."

"You will be careful?"

"Of course." She managed to laugh, though she did not really feel like laughing. The tone of her laughter was tight and high-pitched. "These men will be gone today, and it will be over."

The two turned and walked back to the camp. The argument was over, yet not really. There was a barrier between them, and a silent heaviness of the heart that kept them from speaking as they walked. *How long,* she wondered, *will it be until it is really over?*

It was nearly noon when the four Horn-men rode out, very publicly. Many of the People came to wave to them as they departed. It had been a pleasant diversion to have visitors, and to hear their stories. Especially since these were so unique.

Calling Bird did not go out to participate in the farewell. She felt silly, watching from hiding, and was angry with herself over it. But she refused to risk another confrontation with the men who had caused so much grief between her and Tall Bull. Besides, she dreaded facing the tall older man who seemed to be their leader. His glance last night at the story fire had seemed to reflect more than a passing attention. There was some hidden meaning there, which she did not understand. It sent a chilling sensation creeping up her spine to the back of her neck, where the short neck-hairs seemed to bristle in warning.

She saw the Horn-man turn for a last glance around the village before leaving. She ducked her head, startled, because her instinct told her that he was searching for a last look at *her,* Calling Bird.

Then the visitors were gone, and in the clear autumn sunlight, she felt a little foolish. Surely, there was nothing ominous about these strangers. They had stopped for the night, and the one had looked at her admiringly as a man might be expected to do. Nothing more. It was ridiculous for her to be concerned about it.

Her real concern was the misunderstanding that had risen between her and her long-time friend, Tall Bull. True, there were some doubts. At times she wanted nothing but a lodge of their own, a chance to be with him always and to bear their children. At other times she saw herself as a warrior woman, like Running Eagle, the legendary warrior woman of the Southern band. She had almost decided that such a life was not for her, was merely a young woman's daydream, until recently. She felt that Tall Bull was pushing her a little too fast. They must talk about it seriously, and soon.

Now, there was this new factor. Tall Bull's reaction to the visitors. Unpleasant as the Horn-man's stare had been, her friend's reaction was even more disconcerting. She had never seen the anger and jealousy that he had exhibited this morning. It was a new side of Tall Bull, one she was not certain that she liked at all. Maybe she had teased him too much . . . no, it was more than that. There was a barrier here. Would the rest of her life be spent worrying about what Tall Bull would do each time a man gave her a casual glance?

She did not even want to see Tall Bull today. She busied herself with little tasks around the lodge, avoiding contact with him. *I must get away and think,* she told herself.

It was nearly dark before the opportunity came. Shadows were growing long. The pointed likenesses of the lodges crept across the meadow like dark spears of grass, and up the slope beyond. She could see them grow, pouring purple patches of shade into every low spot in the rolling valley. Sun Boy was painting himself to cross beyond Earth's rim. It was the sort of sunset that she loved to share with Tall Bull. Maybe . . .

"Bird, would you bring some wood?" her mother called.

"Of course, Mother!"

She was gone in an instant. It would be, at least, a chance to be alone for a little while. That would be good, to think quietly. And maybe Tall Bull would come looking for her.

She made her way upstream. There was a big fallen cottonwood where some fuel might still be available. Besides, it was out of sight of the lodges. She and Tall Bull had once spent a pleasant time there.

She arrived, glanced around the clearing, and turned her attention to the tree. The dead giant was silvery-gray in the fading light, its trunk nearly as thick as she was tall. Most of the smaller branches had been broken off already for the cooking fires of the People. She managed to break off one, as long as her arm and as thick. She wondered whether this was as good a source of fuel as she thought. Still, it was a good place to come, and she kept thinking that there was a possibility that Tall Bull might join her. She hoped so. She was ready to apologize, and try to restore the understanding which they had shared.

There was a soft footstep behind a clump of willow. *Ah, he is here!* she thought happily.

"Bull! I am glad . . ."

She broke off in mid-sentence, because the shadowy figure who stepped from behind the willows was not Tall Bull, but one of the Horn-men.

She turned to run, and was confronted by another. From the corner of her eye she saw another rushing forward.

Later, she wished that she had thought to cry out for help, but that was not her nature. She turned to fight. The first attacker went down under a swinging blow from her cottonwood stick. Before she could draw back for another swing, she was grasped from behind, her makeshift weapon wrenched from her grasp. Someone clapped a hand roughly over her mouth. She bit it, and her attacker cuffed her across the side of the head. They fell to the ground in the scuffle, rolling around as she bit and scratched and clawed. She kicked one man in the groin and saw him double in pain.

Then it was over. Her arms and legs were held firmly, and someone had shoved something into her mouth to keep her from crying out. She tried to struggle, but it was useless. Quickly, they tied her wrists and ankles. One tossed her bodily over his shoulder and they hurried away.

Not until they were beyond the ridge did they pause, panting from exertion. The men were talking quietly yet excitedly among themselves in their own tongue. She could understand none of it.

Finally their leader, the man who had stared at her, moved to stand over her where she had been unceremoniously dumped. It was nearly dark now, but she could see clearly as he signed.

"Do not be afraid. You will not be hurt."

That did little to reassure her, however. She was immediately picked up, tossed over a warrior's shoulder again, and they hurried on.

Aiee, she thought, *where is Tall Bull?* Maybe he had come looking for her, and they had killed him. The thought of that was almost as bad as the thought of what might lie ahead for her.

9
>> >> >>

It was well past dark when Tall Bull stopped before the lodge of Calling Bird's parents.

"*Ah-koh*, Uncle," he greeted her father respectfully.

The older man was seated, half reclining against his willow backrest while he enjoyed a pipe before retiring. The chill of night was coming on, and he drew his robe around him against the crisp night air. A small fire burned in front of him, lending light as well as the warmth that comforted his lame left knee, shattered long ago in a fall from a horse.

"*Ah-koh*, Tall Bull. What is it?"

"Uncle, I would speak with your daughter."

At this point a woman thrust her head out of the doorway.

"Bird is not with you?"

"No . . . I have not seen her."

"*Aiee!* I sent her for wood, before dark. When she did not return, I thought you were together."

The young man paused, confused. The tone of this conversation was a trifle accusing, as well as concerned.

"No, not since this morning. She has not been here?"

"Not since dark. Tell me, Bull, do you know what is wrong with her? She was not herself today." There was genuine concern in the voice of Oak Leaf now.

"I . . . I do not know," the young man stammered. "We argued, a little."

"You *argued?*"

"Yes . . . a quarrel . . . I came to try to fix it."

"Aiee!" exclaimed Oak Leaf. "Is she with someone else?"

"I think not . . . she was angry at *me.* And, I with her, maybe."

"Angry with her? What had she done?"

Tall Bull hesitated.

"Nothing, maybe. I thought she was flirting with those men . . . the visitors. She smiled at one of them."

"This morning?"

"No, at the story fire."

Now Young Bear, the girl's father, re-entered the conversation.

"Wait, Bull . . . she showed attention to these visitors?"

"No . . . not really, Uncle." This was an embarrassing thing. "It was probably nothing. I was angry that she smiled at him."

"Tall Bull, could she have gone to follow this man?"

"I think not. He was an older man."

"That one? Their leader? She smiled at *him?"*

"Yes . . . well, he was watching her. I did not think it was good."

"And so it was not, Bull." The older man knocked ashes from his pipe and sat forward.

"I did not trust that one . . . *any* of them. They are not what they seem," said Tall Bull.

"What do you mean, Bull?"

"They did not appear to be traders."

"But they said . . ." Oak Leaf began.

"I know what they said," Tall Bull interrupted, "but there were many things not right. The knives they carried . . ."

"Knives?" asked Bear. "What of them?"

"Uncle," answered the young man respectfully, "some of my friends have metal knives, and I, too, wish to have one. So, I have looked at them, handled them."

"Yes, go on."

"Well, knives are of different sorts. Most of those that the People have came from our trade in Santa Fe, before the war stopped it."

"But there is trade there again."

"Yes. But the knives the Horn People carried are different . . . the shape more slender. Do they not trade with the French in their own territory?"

"So it is said. You think . . ."

"I do not know, Uncle. But maybe the knives they showed us were not from Santa Fe."

"Yes . . ." Young Bear pondered. "Their steel fire-strikers, too . . . shaped differently from those some of our people carry. If they were not what they said, what purpose . . . ?"

There was dead silence as the significance of this conversation sank into the thoughts of the three. Tall Bull was first to voice the concern of them all.

"Could Calling Bird have been *stolen?*"

Such a thing had not happened for many seasons. It had once been not uncommon, the raiding of the People for their tall, long-legged girls for wives. But usually, such activity had been limited to the stealing of children. And none in recent years. Of course, a chance to steal a ripe young girl, flowering to womanhood might be quite tempting. Still . . .

"Something is wrong, here," the older man pondered. "If they wanted a girl, why not a younger child? It would be easier."

"Maybe they want her just for now," suggested Tall Bull, his voice tight at the mere thought.

"No, there is something else," her father said slowly. "If they only wanted a woman, it would have been simpler than this."

"You mean, Uncle, that they chose Calling Bird especially?"

"I do not know. The ways of the Horn People are strange. Maybe . . . *aiee*, maybe Bird only spends the night in the lodge of one of her woman-friends because she is angry at you. Who knows?"

"I do," snapped her mother. "Calling Bird would have told me. Now what are you going to do?"

"I will follow them," stated Tall Bull.

Young Bear looked at his misshapen leg. "You will need help, my son; help I cannot give. Go and talk to her brother. Running Otter will help you."

Tall Bull started to answer that he needed no one, that he and he alone would follow the four and rescue his wife-to-be. His better judgment overcame the idea, and he answered tightly.

"It is good, Uncle. I will go there now."

Running Otter was an ideal man to approach for help in such an emergency. In addition to being a brother of the missing girl, Otter was one of the most respected hunters and able warriors in the Northern band. Even though roused from his sleep, he listened intently to Tall Bull's story, and then nodded decisively.

"We will start at daylight. Not a big party. You, me
. . . we will need a tracker. Yes . . . Spotted Cat." He
was tossing his robe around his shoulders even as he
spoke. "Come, we will talk to him. Then to the holy
man for his prayer chant."

"Do we need others?" Tall Bull blurted. This was
happening so quickly.

"No, I think not. A big party would be harder to
conceal. But we will ask the holy man. Now, a few
supplies . . . horses . . ."

At first light of dawn the three were outside the
camp. Hardly anyone was stirring yet. Spotted Cat
knelt and studied the ground, seemingly lost in thought
as he moved slowly around the clearing in widening
circles. Finally he motioned the others to him.

"It is as you say," he told Tall Bull. "Four men. They
waited here, a long time. A struggle there, the girl
carried . . . probably tied . . . that way. She fought
hard!" he chuckled.

"How do you know that?" Tall Bull demanded, an-
gered at the chuckle.

"This club." He pointed to a cottonwood stick as
thick as his wrist. "Blood on it, blood on the ground. A
piece of fringe, pulled from a legging . . . yes, she
fought!"

"But that could be *her* blood!" Tall Bull insisted,
alarmed.

The wizened little tracker looked at him for a moment, and then spoke. Unexpectedly, his tone was quite
gentle.

"Tall Bull, you must believe that she is all right. Do
not torture yourself. Listen: They want her alive, for
whatever purpose. They would not take her by club-
bing her down with that." He pointed to the club. "No,
they will treat her well, and we will find her."

Running Otter clasped a reassuring hand on the young man's shoulder as he stepped toward the horses. The three rode out, Spotted Cat in the lead.

It was not quite so reassuring when they found the place where Calling Bird's captors were joined by perhaps ten horsemen. Apparently the four Horn-men had rejoined their main party.

"They probably brought a horse for the girl," Spotted Cat observed. "Well planned. I do not understand it all. At least, the tracking is easy."

The heart of Tall Bull was very heavy, as he followed Spotted Cat to the northeast.

Calling Bird lay in the middle of the circle, surrounded by the Horn-men. She was tied hand and foot, but the choking mouth-gag had been removed. They were far from the camp of the People now, and no one could hear her cries for help. At this point, to cry out would only be to lose her dignity, and she refused to give them that satisfaction.

There was no fire. It was obvious that her captors did not want to be seen. They expected to be followed, then. Their expectations were correct on that . . . at least she hoped so. She could not think otherwise. Surely, Tall Bull would try to follow them. That in turn made her anxious. He would not realize that he followed not four, but about fifteen heavily armed warriors.

It had been a terrible blow to her hopes, when her four captors had come to a brushy ravine and had paused to sound a cry like that of a night-bird. Almost at once, a number of horsemen emerged from hiding, leading horses for those who held her. There was a horse for her, too. A strange thing. What could this be? Such a plan . . . it seemed that this entire party and its plans revolved around her. She looked at the warriors in the dim light, their strange horn-like top-knots silhouetted against the starry sky. She did not know their customs, but she feared the worst. For what purpose would a group of men steal a woman, except for one? Was she to be bedded by *all* of these? She shuddered at the thought. There was one ray of hope. The man who seemed to be the leader, the one who had looked at her so strangely by the story fire. He seemed to have not only authority, but special interest in her. Was she to be *his* wife? But surely, a party of this size, this planning, would not be simply for the purpose of stealing a woman for one man. Unless, of course, he was a very special leader of some sort. This man certainly did not show evidence of any superiority of any kind. He was actually very plain and undistinguished-looking.

But there must be something. Actually, even after the roughness of her capture, he seemed concerned for her welfare. Not for her comfort, to be sure. She had been tied tightly, and when she was placed on the horse, both the animal and the prisoner were fastened to this man's person by long cords of rawhide. There would be no escape.

They traveled rapidly northeast until just before dawn, and then took refuge in a shallow but heavily-timbered canyon. The entire party dismounted and prepared for camp. There were many admiring glances, but no overt approaches. She was lifted from the horse, and gently placed on a spread buffalo robe. Her captor approached and stood over her. *Does it happen now?* she wondered, *before all these others, in daylight?*

The man stooped and tied her ankles, and then stood again.

"I am Hunts-Well," he signed. "You will not be hurt,

but are to be honored. I will tell you more later, but for now, you will wear this."

He took from his pouch a beaded amulet on a thong, and placed it around her neck. She said nothing, though the mouth-gag had been removed some time earlier. They could not understand her anyway, and the things she had to say to this man would only be effective if he understood how vile they were. When her hands were freed, maybe, so that she could sign. She glared at him, and then moved to look at the amulet that dangled at her breast. There was something familiar about it . . . the design . . . She had seen it before. One familiar to the People, though not often used. A cross, its arms somewhat thicker at the tips . . . like a four-armed star. A star! Yes, the sign of the Morning Star. But why? What did this have to do with her?

She looked back at the man who stood over her. Hunts-Well, he had called himself. What was his part in this?

"Sleep now," he signed as he covered her with the robe. Then he turned away.

10
>> >> >>

Mountain knew that he had been chosen for the abduction partly because of his strength and quickness. It was a superb honor to have been given the responsibility of carrying the bound Morning Star Princess. He would have thought that Hunts-Well would reserve that task for himself. But as he thought about it, he realized that it was a good choice. Of all the party, he, Mountain, had the greatest power in arms and shoulders. That would be the best way to pick up the girl and make a quick departure.

No matter that old Hunts-Well had never amounted to much. His medicine was strong now, since the Morning Star vision. The others had marveled to themselves that such a man could lead them unerringly across many days of travel, directly to the girl chosen by Morning Star. And the abduction had gone well.

On the second day of travel, Mountain began to relax somewhat. There seemed to be no pursuit. At least, none was evident. They would continue to watch the back trail closely, but it was possible to turn more attention to the comfort and welfare of the captive. It was possible, even, that there was to be no pursuit at all.

He had seen the conflict between this young woman and her would-be suitor, there at the fire. It was apparently a jealousy, a resentment on the part of the young man, and she had been teasing him about it. Such a disagreement would be well known to the rest of the band. The girl had disappeared, quietly and without notice . . . at least, he thought that the abduction had been carried out without anyone's realization. Her people might easily assume that she had left of her own free will, after a lovers' quarrel. It might be assumed, even, that she had followed the visitors. Women did make such choices, and if she did so, it was no concern of anyone's. In that case, they had only to fear pursuit by the rejected lover. He would be no problem to the war party of Horn People, but they would watch for him.

The captive was adjusting well to the situation. She was not happy about it, of course. That would come later, possibly. But Mountain already admired her courage and resiliency. She was like the willow, which bends in the wind but does not break. A stronger tree than the willow might be broken in a storm, trying to defy the force of the wind, but the willow bends, gives way, and then returns to its upright stance.

Yes, this girl was much like the willow. The way she moved, the motion of her shapely legs and body as she walked. He had never seen a woman quite so desirable, he thought. He had felt the curves of her body against him when he tossed her over his shoulder. She had been tied and helpless, but it was so distracting, even in the excitement of the moment, to feel her warmth. It would be pleasure beyond belief to lie with such a woman.

Now he lay in his sleeping-robe, fighting such thoughts. It was unthinkable, of course, and a wave of guilt swept over him. The girl must remain pure, for she was the property of Morning Star. But it was hard to ignore the demands of his body. And surely, the girl must have felt some attraction for him. Had she not smiled at him at the fire that night? At least, he thought so.

He lay and listened to the regular breathing of those around him. Especially, the breathing of the captive, who lay in the center of the circle of sleeping warriors. The robes of Plenty-Snows were empty, as he was on watch outside the camp.

The soft breath-sounds of the sleeping girl were having a profound effect on Mountain. He began to imagine how exciting it might be to lie in one's own lodge and hear that soft whisper in his ear. Maybe he could move closer to her and no one would notice. She might appreciate the warmth he could provide, for the night was frosty. He did not move, however, for fear held him back. The girl was taboo, the property of the deity.

He tossed restlessly, and turned over, but his fantasies still tortured him. It seemed a shame, almost . . . a waste, that such a desirable creature as the woman who slept there would never warm the bed of a man. Of Morning Star, of course, but it was hard to visualize that union. Again, he felt guilty for even questioning it. This was necessary, he knew, to provide a new bride for Morning Star so that the corn would grow. At least, so said old Hawk's Tail, the Morning Star Priest.

Mountain sighed deeply. For the good of his people, he must help to protect this girl, the Morning Star Princess. If something happened to her purity before they reached the village, their mission was a failure. Hunts-Well would have to start over.

Suddenly an idea occurred to him. A moon ago, there had been no Princess. If something happened, would there not be another selection? Of course! If the purity of the captive no longer existed, she would be of no use to Morning Star. And no use to Hunts-Well and his party.

Maybe he, Mountain, could convince the girl to lie with him. Then he could not only have that pleasure, but it would free her of the obligation to Morning Star. But how could he talk to her? She understood none of their tongue, but did understand hand-signs. He had seen Hunts-Well talking to her very briefly a time or two. Still, it would take much sign-talk to convince her. He did not see how it could be done. Maybe a little at a time . . . a sign or two. But could that be done before they reached home?

Then a bold possibility occurred to him. He could take her by force, suddenly and without warning. Then it would be over, and a new selection would be demanded by Morning Star. Meanwhile, the girl would be free to marry whom she liked. Surely she would favor the attentions of such a bold lover. And after the act, of course, there would be plenty of time to explain what he had done for her. She would probably fly into his arms.

Again, he thought of the softly rounded curves, the warm body against his. He could wait no longer. This might as well be the time.

Very quietly, he lifted his robe and rolled out of its warmth. He waited a little while to assure himself, but there was only the soft breathing of the sleepers. He crawled toward the slim figure in the center of the circle, pausing often to look and listen.

He reached her side, and carefully looked in the dim starlight at the way the buffalo robe was folded around the girl. He must not become entangled in it. Her eyes were closed in slumber, and he paused to enjoy the beauty of her features. He regretted that he would have to cover her mouth at first to keep her from crying out. Her hands were tied, so that would make it easier. He took a last look around, and all seemed calm. There was a gray blur in the eastern sky that predicted the dawn. He must hurry.

He clapped a hand over the mouth of the sleeping girl, holding her down with the other hand and with the weight of his chest and shoulders even as he did so. She struggled helplessly, fighting his advances. He *must* go through with the plan, now.

He flung the sleeping robe aside and smothered her with his weight as she struggled. He could not control her, even with her hands tied. She evaded him, rolling away from his advance. He was dimly aware of some-one approaching, and turned to look.

There was only the space of a heartbeat in which he recognized the face of Hunts-Well, mad with rage. Then he felt something strike his chest as he turned to face his assailant. There was no pain at first, for a mo-ment, and he was surprised to see the knife in the hand of Hunts-Well as he withdrew it to strike again. Hunts-Well grasped his shoulder and spun him aside, striking yet a third time as Mountain fell.

He realized that he was mortally wounded, and tried to explain. His lips moved but there was no sound. And now there was pain, which swept over him in a wave.

"Son of a dog," hissed Hunts-Well, "I should cut your heart out."

Others were running toward them, talking excitedly. It was a strange sensation, as life ebbed away. Dawn was growing lighter, yet his sight grew darker. The last object that his dimming vision saw was the pale yellow of the eastern sky, and the bright reddish glow of the rising Morning Star. *The god will not be denied,* he thought.

The leader bent over her, the rage in his face changing to anxiety. Almost tenderly, he lifted her to a sitting position.

"Are you hurt?" he signed.

Her hands were still tied, but she shook her head. She was puzzled. One of the party had tried to assault her, and the leader had killed him for it. What strange, violent men! Once more, she wondered what was in store for her.

"I will protect you," the man was signing. "You have nothing to fear."

Nothing to fear! The thought would have been amusing if it were not so real. In the past two days she had been abducted, cuffed around, tied, thrown on a horse for punishing travel, and nearly raped. Nothing to fear?

Well, she would try to make the best of it. They would be traveling again soon. Day was nearly here. She held her bound hands up to the leader, trying to look helpless and pleading. If her hands were freed, her chances of escape were better. At least, she could sign, and maybe learn what all this was about.

The leader seemed lost in thought, but finally nodded agreement.

"A little while," he signed. "Do not run; we will catch you."

She nodded, and he removed the thongs.

"Thank you," she gestured, rubbing her chafed wrists. "How are you called, and where do we go?"

"I am your Wolf-man," he answered. "Your protector. I will see that you are not harmed."

"Then let me go."

"No, I cannot. Morning Star has spoken. You are greatly honored. Now, come. We must go."

They were quickly ready to depart. Hunts-Well took the precaution of tying a cord to her wrist, and the other end to his saddle.

"You must not try to escape," he warned.

She shook her head solemnly.

One of the warriors spoke to her captor, pointing to the corpse on the ground. Hunts-Well did not even speak, but gave a derisive hand-sign gesture.

"Let him lie."

Her last glimpse of the man who had attacked her in her bed was of his sightless eyes, staring at the dawn sky with a look of complete surprise.

As she looked back later, Calling Bird could hardly realize how rapidly she had adapted to her abductors' way of thinking. Many captives have done the same, before and since. It must begin in desperation. *I must understand these people, so they will spare me,* the captive thinks, maybe unconsciously. *If I understand him, maybe he will be sympathetic to me, too.*

These men seemed kind and sympathetic from the first. After the physical capture and its necessary roughness, they settled into a much gentler routine. They made it quite clear that there was to be no escape, but she was treated with the utmost of respect. She had the strong impression that any one of these men would gladly die for her, defending her from harm.

They respected her privacy to attend to her bodily needs, and made certain that her bed was comfortable when they stopped each night to rest. Her place was surrounded by the beds of the entire party. The first night, she had realized that it was not their intent to assault her. She assumed that the encircling warriors were placed in that manner to prevent her escape. Before long, however, she realized that this was only part of their purpose. Their main goal seemed to be that of protection, to keep her from harm.

She was given the best of the food available, and if food was scarce for a day or two, her needs were met first. She was embarrassed about that. Among the People, it would have been first the children, then share alike. Among these, she could not understand the favoritism. She was certainly not being regarded as a child.

"You are special," signed Hunts-Well in answer to her signed query. "A blessed one."

"I do not understand," she persisted.

"No matter," he gestured casually. "Later . . . but we are your protectors, to keep you from harm."

Calling Bird did not understand, but it was difficult *not* to be cooperative with people who treated her so well. This made it easier to develop a sort of uneasy trust. She had never lived so well, with no responsibilities, pampered in every possible way. Even the man whom she had struck down in the first attack seemed to hold no resentment. His injured forehead was now healing well. She was almost sorry for her vicious defense.

She continued to inquire in hand-signs, but met with very little information that she had not already been told. Basically, that she was a chosen person, was blessed, and very special. She would be honored, and protected from all harm.

Several times their leader, Hunts-Well, had used a hand-sign that she understood to be similar to that for a Warrior Sister of the People. It held a connotation of respect and high regard. Some of the warriors seemed almost in awe of her, so great was their esteem. This, too, allayed her fears. In a few days she was more relaxed and confident.

She still thought of escape, but there seemed to be no hurry. It was quite tempting to continue this pampered and honored existence. She could escape later if she wished, she told herself. To add to this confidence, her captors seemed to settle into the routine quite comfortably, too.

They encountered one stretch of bad weather. Cold Maker came howling across the prairie, throwing rain and sleet, coating everything with a layer of ice. Her captors were quick to react at the first sign of storm. Quickly, they entered a wooded ravine and began to cut brush for a shelter. It would be small, and it took a little while to realize that it was a shelter for her alone. In a short while she was safely snuggled in, basking in the warmth of a fire before the open side of the lean-to. The others were building more shelters by twos and threes, but it was plain that there would be none like that of the honored Sister, none so tightly constructed or so warm.

They camped there for four days, waiting. Finally Sun Boy overcame the might of Cold Maker and warmed the earth again. The travelers hurried on.

Sometimes she thought of Tall Bull. He must wonder about her. She had fully expected pursuit by the People. Surely her father, too, though unable to participate in a rescue party himself, would urge that it be done. Tall Bull was highly respected by her parents, and they should have planned together, to send a war party in pursuit. Her captors had fully expected it. For several days at first they had carefully watched the back trail.

But there had been no pursuit. Her heart was heavy over this. It said to her that no one cared. She found it hard to accept that Tall Bull would be still holding a grudge in his heart over their silly quarrel. When she had been stolen, he should immediately have come to his senses and started to organize pursuit. Yet there was nothing. She began to resent him for it, a little at first, then more and more. Any feeling that Tall Bull ever had for her must have been quite small, she thought, if he did not even care. She could be dead or enslaved, and Tall Bull had not cared enough to try to plan her rescue.

Another possibility occurred to her. Maybe the People were unaware of her abduction. Tall Bull had accused her of flirting with the visitors at the story fire. Maybe he now assumed that she had eloped with one of the men. He would tell her parents of the quarrel and of his suspicion. They would shake their heads sadly and her mother would cluck her tongue in disapproval, and that would be the end. They would all go back to their normal activities and forget that there was once a headstrong young woman named Calling Bird.

The more she thought along this line, the more resentful she became. They had no right to disregard her so! They should have investigated. When she did not return from gathering wood, someone should have been concerned. At first, her parents might have assumed that she was with Bull. But when they learned, even the next morning, that he had not seen her, *someone* should have investigated. There was plenty of sign there to indicate her abduction, she thought angrily, if anyone had cared enough to look. Her anger and resentment increased.

So, in this strange way, she found herself resenting her family and friends while she had ever more regard for her captors. *At least they are concerned for me,* she thought. *Not like Tall Bull, who does not care.*

She began to regain much of her normal cheerfulness, and she could tell that this pleased her captors. They began to relax, which in turn pleased her. There was still in her mind the idea of escape, but it was not urgent. Maybe some day, she now thought. Meanwhile, she would continue to enjoy this pampering and fine treatment. Let Tall Bull worry a while longer, if he even cared at all. She would show him. Some day, she would return to the People, and flaunt her experiences to them. *I found people who appreciated me,* she would say to Tall Bull.

He would probably cry and beg forgiveness. Maybe she would forgive him, she decided, but not for a while. Let him worry about it. Yes, that was it. Torture him a while, make him worry. Punish him a little for his inconsiderate attitude. Then finally forgive him, and enjoy the kindness that his gratitude would bring. This was a pleasant daydream, and she thought often of how well Tall Bull would treat her after she became his wife.

Meanwhile, she would continue to enjoy the good treatment she now experienced. She settled into the routine of travel; stop for the night or longer, if the weather required, move on . . . There were always "wolves" out in front and behind, and one or two hunting, for the meat to sustain them as they traveled.

Once they stopped at a village of Growers to trade some fresh meat for corn and beans. It varied their diet, and was a pleasant change. The women there were good to her. It was pleasant to see a woman.

"Is one of these your husband?" a woman signed to her.

"No, these are my brothers," she answered, laughing.

The women seemed puzzled, and a little concerned. It was amusing to see. Then Hunts-Well, realizing that they were conversing in sign-talk, hurried her away. He seemed a little angry over the episode.

"I only wished to talk to a woman," she protested.

"But you are special," Hunts-Well signed, his face stern and unyielding. "Stay away from outsiders. There will be women to care for you."

"When?"

"When we reach our village."

"When is that?" she demanded.

"Not long, now. Three, four sleeps. Come, we travel."

Calling Bird mounted her horse, excited and pleased. *Three or four days!* Now, finally, the travel would be over, and she would learn what this was all about.

The next day, three men dismounted and studied the village of the Growers from a distance.

"Is this where they live?" asked Tall Bull.

"I think not," answered the tracker. "The men we follow are Horn People. These are Kenzas, maybe. They might stop here . . ."

"They had that buffalo kill yesterday," Running Otter observed. "Maybe they trade here . . . meat for corn or other supplies?"

Spotted Cat nodded. "I will go around . . . see if I can find their trail."

"Wait!" suggested Otter. "I will ride in, buy some supplies, and see what I can find out."

"It is good," agreed the tracker. He was already pulling the saddle from his horse. "We will let the horses graze. They are getting thin."

It was true. A horse must spend half his day in eating, and they had been traveling hard, with no time to properly care for the animals. Those they followed had the same problem, of course, but not so acutely. The Horn-men were going home. Actually, one of their horses *had* gone lame and had been discarded. Apparently its rider was using the mount of the dead man they had found.

That was a strange thing. Only a few nights out . . . one of the men they pursued, killed by several stab wounds in the stomach and chest. It was a puzzling thing. He had been killed by one of his own, Spotted Cat believed. There was no sign of an attack, no other people in the area. And the dead man appeared to lie where he had fallen, staring at the sky.

"He did a bad thing," Spotted Cat reasoned.

"What . . . why?" asked the puzzled Tall Bull.

"They left him here. Did not prepare his body for burial. Yet they did not hurry to leave. So, they did not *care*. He must have broken one of their taboos. A powerful one."

Now, they waited for the return of Running Otter. Tall Bull was impatient and eager, pacing nervously, but the tracker lay down and was quickly asleep. After what seemed a long time to the waiting Tall Bull, Otter returned. Spotted Cat was instantly awake and on his feet.

"They stopped here," Otter stated as he swung down. "My sister is well. They said she is not tied, and was cheerful. *Aiee*, there is much that I do not understand, here."

"Cheerful?" Tall Bull gasped.

"Yes, so they said."

"Could she be pretending?" Bull demanded.

"Maybe. But it is strange. The women seemed worried about her."

"But they told you she was happy!"

"Yes. That is the strange part. They speak none of our tongue, and I, none of theirs. We talked only in signs, so

I was not sure . . . they kept pointing northeast and making the signs for 'Morning Star' and 'woman.' "

Spotted Cat spread his hands and shrugged his shoulders, puzzled.

"You say they seemed worried for her?"

"Yes, so it seemed."

"Then maybe we should be, also," the tracker admitted. "Let us hurry."

"Oh, yes," Otter said, as they mounted the horses. "They said the Horn People live maybe four sleeps away. Northeast."

12
>> >> >>

Far to the north, in the village of the Horn People, life went on. It was a time of hunger, as had been expected, even though the winter had been mild. A mild winter, of course, was a relative thing. To those who starved or froze to death, a particular winter was the worst ever seen.

It was much like a small skirmish, Bear Paws reflected. Those not directly involved have a tendency to be more objective, to see a difference between a great battle and a mere brush with the enemy. But to those directly involved, those killed and wounded, there are no small battles. One is just as dead, feels just as much pain, and his family mourns as sorrowfully.

He wondered about his own family, back among the Elk-dog People. He had thought of his parents often during his early captivity here. For a while he had wished to get word to them that he was alive, but the opportunity never presented. By the time he had acquired the freedom to do as he wished, he had become so entwined with these people, and with the family of Pretty Sky, now his wife . . . *aiee,* he really *should* try to send word. But travelers going that way were scarce. He could go himself, but did not wish to leave his wife . . . the children were too small to travel. Maybe some day . . .

But the moons and the seasons passed, and the time did not seem right. Then, too, his previous life had seemed less and less important as he became one of the Horn People. Occasionally he thought, with some degree of guilt, that his parents must think him dead. Even that softened after a while. They would have mourned him and forgotten him long ago, he tried to tell himself. He was not completely able to accept this excuse for himself, but it helped.

At least, it had until recently. Last autumn, the entire village had become emotional over the Morning Star Vision. Visions were important, of course, but the purpose of this one, the entire idea of the bride for their deity, Morning Star . . . How long had it been now, since the search party had departed? Several moons. It had been the Moon of Madness when Hunts-Well had been chosen. An odd time to begin a journey, with winter coming. But, their quest took them southward, how far no one knew. Maybe the weather would be warmer.

He counted on his fingers . . . the Moon of Dark Nights, the Moon of Snows (though there had been few this season), and now the Moon of Hunger. The Hunger Moon had been almost a misnomer among his own people. There was an oft-repeated joke that it needed a new name. It was his understanding that before the People had the horse there had been much starvation in winter, when food ran out. There were stories of old people walking out into the open prairie in a snow-storm, proudly singing the Death Song. There they would battle Cold Maker to the death, cheerfully. In this way they could know that there would be food for the children, and after all, children were the future of the People.

Among these, his wife's people, it was quite different. There were the summer and fall hunts for buffalo, but the entire world did not depend on buffalo, here. There were crops, especially the corn. But the last season or two, with both the hunt and the crops scarce, there was much hunger. He wondered if the People had felt the strain of the poor year, too.

All this, maybe, had made him think more about his parents, his brother, his friends. Then, too, Pretty Sky seemed to have changed. It was at about the time of the Morning Star Vision, he thought. She had not wanted to speak of that, and in avoiding it, had placed a distance between them. Then the discussion or two about their friend whose wife was also occasionally a wife for his brother. He did not understand that at all, though no one else seemed to think anything of it. Yet, Pretty Sky appeared somehow to resent his non-understanding. That concerned him. He did not want her to think that he was criticizing the customs of her people, yet did not want her to think he accepted them, either. For he could not accept what to him seemed like infidelity.

This had driven them farther apart. Maybe this was one reason that he was thinking more often of his homeland, his parents.

Now, it was nearly time for the Moon of Awakening. Already, there were signs. Swelling buds on the willows, an occasional warm sunny day to tempt a person with the smells of moist earth under the cold surface. With all of this, he wondered what had happened to the

Morning Star party. Should they not be returning? The Morning Star Ceremony was a springtime festival, Red Hand had said. If they did not return soon, it might be too late to prepare for the ceremony at the proper position of the stars. He rather hoped so, he had to admit. The whole idea of giving a girl to Morning Star was revolting to him.

Maybe the mission had been a failure. It was possible that the party had perished on the winter prairie. At this thought he felt a pang of guilt. He did not really want their quest to fail, at least not that way. *Aiee*, sometimes he became so confused . . . what *did* he want?

One thing seemed certain. If the party had survived, they would soon be returning, to report their success or lack thereof. He wondered what would happen if they had been unsuccessful. Would they even return, to report to the Morning Star Priest that they had failed? He would, himself, find it very difficult to report his failure to such a completely domineering figure as Hawk's Tail, who held the mystical powers of Morning Star.

In the back of his mind, another uneasy thought stirred from time to time. If they were successful, and returned from their quest with a girl who would be the Bride of the Star, who might it be? It was hard to think of such a figure, who would become the Princess, honored, worshipped, pampered, and finally sacrificed, as a real person. She was like the imaginary figures in the tales around the story fires. Would she know the entire significance of the Morning Star pageantry? If so, how would she ever consent to participate? For that matter, how would a girl from another tribe ever consent to leave her people and accompany Hunts-Well and his party anyway?

Well, no matter, he decided. He would have nothing

to do with any of it. The less he knew and saw, the better. Maybe the corn crop *would* be good, maybe the strange barrier between him and Pretty Sky would be removed. He hoped so. Their present relationship was quite uncomfortable.

Bear Paws' first hint of the returning party was a shout from the village. He had gone on foot to hunt in the next valley. He was spending more time away from the village now, because of the questions in his own mind, and because it was quite uncomfortable now to be with Sky. They seemed to be growing farther apart each day.

One extra advantage of his time spent in hunting was, of course, that he was sometimes successful. This was not one of those times. The area had been hunted intensively, and small game was depleted in number. He saw only one squirrel, and it was wary, quickly disappearing into a brushy cleft. There were no rabbits at all.

His best chance was at a deer, which he encountered quite unexpectedly. He did not expect to see a deer, because this thin strip of timber had been hunted so intensively. He was moving slowly and carefully, looking for rabbits in the tall dry grass, when he saw a movement ahead. The doe was browsing quietly, and seemed unaware of his presence. She was broadside to him, about twenty paces away, head lowered, the tail hanging down in the position that indicates no alarm. Very slowly he raised the bow, and drew his arrow to the head. It was already fitted to the string. He concentrated on the spot just behind the left shoulder. When the animal took her next step, that leg would shift, moving the upper leg forward to expose the area over the heart. *Wait, now . . . not yet . . .* As the doe stepped forward, she raised her head. Maybe some animal sense warned her, maybe it was just a thing that happened, but she looked toward the stalker. The bowstring twanged just as the white flag of the tail flew upward in reflex warning. The deer leaped forward, the arrow buzzed harmlessly past her, and she was gone. Even worse, the misguided shot shattered one of Bear Paws' best arrows on a stone outcrop beyond.

Discouraged, he turned back toward the village. There would again be hunger in the lodge tonight. Anyway, he knew that there was at least one deer in the area. With spring coming, they would be moving around, and he could return here again.

He was just topping the rise above the village when he heard the shout. Instinctively, he fitted an arrow to his bow and hurried forward. Was there trouble?

But no, this was a shout of joy! He could see the riders, faces daubed with black paint to indicate success in their mission. They were splashing across the riffle and into the village. Even at this distance he could see that one of the riders, carefully surrounded by the others, was a woman. A tall, graceful woman in light-colored buckskins, who sat her horse well.

As he hurried down the slope, people began to gather, following the returning procession, staring in awe at the girl who would be the Morning Star Princess. They stopped before the lodge of Hawk's Tail, and the priest stepped out to greet them, hand raised in greeting.

Bear Paws stopped, panting from his hurry, and looked over the heads of the crowd. The girl was beautiful, her face calm and poised, even in these circumstances. Her hands were not tied, and he marveled at how they had persuaded her to come with them. She did not know, of course . . . how could she?

She tossed her head, throwing the long plaited locks of hair back over her shoulders. There was something familiar . . . he could not know this woman, but . . . Suddenly it came to him. The cut and decoration of the buckskin dress, the pattern of her moccasins, the plait of her hair.

Aiee! This girl was one of his own! The captive who would be given to Morning Star was a woman of *his* nation, the Elk-dog People.

13
>> >> >>

Bear Paws watched with interest while people emptied the lodge that had been chosen for the dwelling of the Morning Star Princess. It was, of course, one of the largest and newest in the village. Every piece of personal property must be removed, Red Hand had told him. The lodge would become taboo for all but those who were assigned the responsibility of caring for the honored young woman, and those involved in the ceremonies.

Four women were chosen to meet every need of the bride-to-be, cooking the finest foods for her, combing her hair, dressing her in the soft ceremonial buckskin dresses. She would eat from a sacred wooden bowl, handed down through generations of Morning Star priests.

Her protector, or Wolf-man, would be Hunts-Well, who had been taken from his family by reason of his vision. He would not return home until after the coming events. At all times he would be responsible for the safety of the girl. The women might take a time of relief while the others attended the lodge, but the Wolf-man was constantly on guard. He would sleep inside the entrance of the lodge, and any intruder must approach the honored bride *over* his body.

The ceremonies themselves would last for four days, Red Hand related, culminating in the pre-dawn ritual on the fifth morning.

"When does it begin?" asked Bear Paws. He swallowed hard against the tightness in his throat.

"No one knows. It will be announced. But only the Morning Star Priest can tell. He watches the Star, and Morning Star tells him. I have heard that it appears ringed with red when it rises."

Bear Paws did not reply. This entire situation was beyond his understanding, completely foreign to all that his own people stood for. Even Sun himself would not demand the life of a maiden. Bear Paws had struggled with the idea earlier, when old Hawk's Tail called for a Morning Star Vision. He had tried with a great deal of success to enter into the ways of his wife's people. Surely his shaved head and horn-swept scalplock were evidence of his sincerity.

There had even been a time when he decided that he could adjust to the procurement and sacrifice of the Morning Star Maiden. He would never approve, but it was, after all, not his doing, not his religion, but that of the Horn People. If he could only avoid contact with any of it, remain completely detached until it was over . . . Maybe he could go on a lone hunt, and not return until after the ceremonies.

That had been before the return of the search party, before he had seen the girl, and realized that she was one of his own. Now, he had even greater problems.

Even though she seemed willing, and was cooperating with her captors, he was certain that it was because she did not understand . . . did not know how this series of events was to end. If he could only talk to her . . . This seemed highly unlikely, if Red Hand's description of the coming ceremonial days and nights proved accurate. The girl would be guarded every moment.

Bear Paws wondered, of course, who the girl might be. She was young and extremely beautiful. He did not recognize her, but she would have changed much since he left the People, five seasons ago. There might have been much change in her appearance since then. He tried to visualize how she might have looked at the age of ten or eleven, when he had last seen her. If, of course, he had *ever* seen her. There would have been hundreds of young girls this age, and he would have paid little attention to any of them at that time.

She was probably of the Northern band, he decided. Possibly the Eastern band, but the nearest and most logical for the search party to have contacted would have been the Northern. His own was the Southern band, of course, another reason that he might not know this girl. And, she would have changed so very much. The slim long legs had attained the attractive shape that was a matter of great pride for the women of the People. The soft curves of the breasts pushed gently against yielding buckskin. It was impossible for him to imagine that anyone could wish to still this vibrant life . . . *Aiee!* He must stop such thoughts. He was making himself crazy.

What could he do? There seemed nothing at all. Yet the picture in his mind, the thought of this tall proud young woman, unaware of her fate . . . He did not see how he could accept this situation, and his heart was very heavy. Maybe the lone hunt that he had considered earlier . . .

Worst of all, this was destroying his relationship with his wife. He did not quite understand that. They had always been able to talk of their problems. By hand-signs, even before he had learned her language. Time spent in each other's arms always seemed to make things better.

Until now . . . He did not think that he had withdrawn from her. He had tried his best to ask her about the Morning Star Vision, and all that it entailed. Her answers were short and curt, and she seemed to resent him for asking.

After the party of Hunts-Well had departed, he had hoped for a better relationship, a reconciliation of some sort, but it did not happen. If anything, their relationship continued to worsen. She seemed to avoid him, and turned away his questions.

"Is it the Morning Star?" he finally asked.

She looked at him long and hard, and finally her expression softened, though only a little.

"Maybe," she agreed. "You cannot understand all of our ways."

But why should she resent him for that? She had known that, from the first . . .

"Do you sometimes think you should not have saved me when I was captured?" he asked seriously.

They had joked of this, early in their marriage. Now, it was not a joke. He saw tears come to her eyes. She shook her head, but did not answer. She rose and hurried away. He felt farther from her than ever. They had become strangers, and he wondered if they could ever again have the understanding that they once had. Surely not, he thought, unless they could speak of this thing that had come between them, the Morning Star.

• • • •

The days passed, and tension mounted. The Morning Star Princess was seldom seen. Only occasionally was she taken outside for a short while to enjoy the freshness of a warm sunny day. She was carefully surrounded by the women who were her attendants and guarded by the heavily-armed Wolf-man.

Springtime was awakening now. Long lines of geese honked their way northward to wherever it was that they would build summer lodges and raise young, far in a distant land. Bear Paws envied them. The great birds could fly free to less threatening places. He wondered what springtime might be like in the northern prairies and lakes where they would summer. Maybe he could follow them . . .

He watched from a distance as the unsuspecting captive came out of her earth-lodge for a walk. She was not allowed contact with the people of the village during these outings. The girl seemed cheerful and happy, talking in hand-signs to her attendants. She was wearing a beautifully-decorated dress of white buckskin, which accented the graceful lines of her figure. Her dark hair was pulled back from her face, showing well her strong features. On her forehead he could see the symbol of Morning Star. She would wear this painted emblem until the morning when . . . *aiee,* how could he allow this thing to happen?

The girl raised her arms high and drew in a great breath of the fresh air of springtime, exhaling with a small cry of pure joy. This would be the last springtime in which she would do so, thought Bear Paws. He clenched his fists in anguish. There was a strong temptation to rush forward and shout a warning to her, tell her that she must run. But he knew it would be useless. She would be quickly overpowered by her attendants, and would then be confronted with days of anguish until the fateful morning. No, let her enjoy her days and the honor she now received. At least, for now. He might yet think of a way to help her.

He wished that he might talk with his brother, Red Horse. Red Horse was a holy man, a man of vision. He would know how to proceed. *Red Horse, help me,* Bear Paws thought. Still, he had an uncomfortable feeling that possibly his brother would not be of help. If they could talk, Red Horse might tell him to mind his own troubles, that this was no concern of his. He could almost hear the accusing tones of his brother's voice: *This is what you chose, to become one of the Horn People. You must live with it.* Such thoughts were of no help.

The Morning Star Princess and her attendants finished their walk and reentered the lodge. Bear Paws turned away, heavy of heart. He did not wish to go to his own lodge yet. There was only more hurt there. He went on foot, carrying his bow as a pretense, but his mind was not on the hunt. He needed to be alone, though being alone did not seem to help, either. He wanted to run, run away from the doubts and hurt and concern for the girl in that fateful earth-lodge.

He walked northward for some distance, choosing that direction for no better reason than that of the high-flying geese. Finally he stopped and sat watching the colors of the sunset. It was not the brilliant gold and red of autumn sunsets, but it was beautiful to see, anyway. It brought him a sense of calm. In the immensity of sun and sky and prairie, his own being seemed small, his problems unimportant. He watched until it was nearly dark, and the night-creatures began to stir.

It was growing cool, and it suddenly struck him that it was ridiculous to try to run away. He was unprepared for a journey anyway. He rose, established his directions by the Real-star as it appeared in the north, then turned his back on it and headed back. He realized that he still had no answer to his problems, but at least felt better about them.

It was late when he entered the lodge and found his way to his sleeping robes. The fire in the center of the lodge had burned down to a few coals which offered little light. Pretty Sky was sound asleep. At least it seemed so, and he was glad. He did not want to talk tonight.

14

》》 》 》 》

There were times when Tall Bull did not know whether he would be able to continue. During the long days in slow pursuit of the Horn People, it was very hard to restrain himself. The very thought that Calling Bird was ahead there, a prisoner of the strange warriors from the north . . . *aiee,* his heart was heavy.

Spotted Cat assured him repeatedly that all was well with her. The old tracker had, several times, crept up to the abductors' camp in the darkness and observed them, unseen. It seemed certain that the girl's captors did not realize that they were followed. They were actually careless about placing guards, he reported to the others.

"Then let us steal her away at night!" urged Tall Bull.

"No," Spotted Cat insisted, "she is watched closely, and sleeps in the center of the circle. She will not be harmed, Bull."

"Then why did they take her? I do not understand!"

"Nor do I," the tracker answered, "but whatever it is will not happen as they travel, and for now, she is safe."

"But should we not try to free her before they reach their own people and the safety of their village?" Tall Bull persisted.

"Think, Bull!" Running Otter argued. "There are fifteen of them. Well, fourteen, since they killed the one. But, suppose you did reach her and free her. They are many, and we do not know the country. We could not escape."

Tall Bull's head told him that this was true, but his heart still protested. There must be something that they could do. The entire situation seemed so strange, so unreal.

"There is much here that we do not understand," continued Otter. "We must learn what it is about, first. Spotted Cat can do that."

"But . . ." Tall Bull was still unconvinced.

"Look," said the tracker. "You would not crawl into a bear's den without first knowing whether the bear was inside. We must watch and learn."

They had discovered one good means to learn of those they pursued. It had worked well when they first tried it. Now, they did not hesitate to ride boldly into a village of growers and offer meat to trade. When, of course, they were able to make a kill. Then, during their stay, they would casually gossip in hand-signs about the party which had passed this way.

Running Otter proved quite adept at this, jokingly speaking of his sister who had eloped with someone.

"You follow to get her back?" one of their hosts asked.

Otter managed to laugh uproariously, as if this had not occurred to him.

"No, no! Whoever he was, she is now his problem!"

There was laughter, and Otter carried his thrust a step further.

"We only happen to go the same direction," he went on. "If we do encounter them, I will give her man my sympathy."

It was much different after they were back on the trail.

"We must be more careful," Running Otter said. "Not ask so much."

Spotted Cat grunted in agreement. Another thing was of great concern to Tall Bull. The tracker, in assuring him that the girl was doing well, mentioned that she was not tied, and was being treated well. Why, Bull wondered, did she act in this way? She should be resisting her captors in every way she could, making things more difficult for *them.* At least, up to the point that it was unsafe to do so. Instead, according to the description given by Spotted Cat, the girl was actually cooperating. She must be, otherwise she would still be tied.

This led to a gnawing doubt in the mind of the young suitor. He had been jealous of Bird's reaction to the visitors when they stopped in the camp of the People. He had accused her of flirtation. *Aiee,* that seemed long ago, now! He had realized that such a charge was ridiculous, and was ashamed of it, later. But, now . . . could it have been true? Was there one among her captors who had taken the flirtation seriously, and had induced the others to help him kidnap the girl? That would buy time for such a man to court her, to bring her around to agreement. Tall Bull was frustrated, knowing that he might find it easier to understand if he knew the marriage customs of the Horn People.

"Did she appear to be with any one man?" he asked the tracker.

The wizened little man chuckled, then became serious, seeing the concern in Tall Bull's face.

"No," he said gently. "Bull, I see your worry. It is not good to think of your woman with another man. But it is not so. They all treat her well, but . . . well, with *honor.*"

"Why, Uncle? This makes no sense to me!"

Spotted Cat spread his hands in a puzzled gesture.

"Who knows what Horn People think? They are different, Bull. We will find out, but for now, you must know that Calling Bird is well treated. And, that she sleeps with none of them!"

That assurance helped some, but it was still difficult.

Finally came the time when it seemed that they must be nearing the region which the Horn People called home. Their attitude was different, Spotted Cat reported after one of his nocturnal forays. They seemed to possess an air of confidence, a feel for the spirit of the country they now traveled.

"We must be careful, now," the tracker reported. "They are nearing home."

"How far?" Tall Bull asked quickly.

"Who knows?" shrugged Cat. "I only feel that they are at home here."

"Can we ask growers?" Running Otter wondered.

"Maybe. But we must be careful. The Horn People are growers."

"But they hunt, too," Otter reminded. "They are different from the Growers we know."

"What do you mean?" Spotted Cat asked.

"Well, it is said that Horn People live in earth-lodges. We have seen none of those. Let us find a town of lodges made of poles and grass, like the last one we visited, and ask them."

"Ask them what?"

"Ask of the Horn People. Tell them that Horn-men visited our winter camp and we exchanged stories . . ."

"Yes," nodded the tracker. "Maybe so. They invited our people to visit, and now we do so, we will say. And ask the way to the town of our new friends! It is good!"

They sat around the fire, making small talk in hand-signs, about the weather, the mild winter, the hunting . . . They had been fortunate enough to encounter a small band of deer, and had managed to kill a fat yearling. The gift of meat might open hearts and loosen tongues.

"We have heard of your Elk-dog People," the leader of the host village signed. "We are honored by your visit."

Tall Bull wondered if these growers would have been so honored if they came asking for food instead of bringing it.

"It pleases us to be here," Otter signed.

"Why do you travel here?" the old chief asked.

Otter spread his palms.

"Why do geese fly north?" he asked.

Now would be the time . . .

"Some Horn People visited us this past winter," Otter went on. "They told us of their land, and asked us to visit. Can you tell us where they make their lodges?"

"Of course!" The old man pointed. "A big town . . . earth-lodges."

"So they said. You have been there?"

The chief nodded.

"When I was younger. I do not travel much now. My bones ache."

Otter nodded sympathetically.

"I can understand. How will we find them?"

"On the river. Go straight north, then follow downstream. You should find it easily. And, another thing! You are fortunate . . . They have a new Morning Star Princess. Maybe they will have their ceremony while you are there!"

The three visitors had been ready to leave, but now settled back, trying hard to appear casual.

"Tell us of this ceremony, my chief!" signed Otter. "It is unknown to us."

The old man smiled, pleased at the interest shown by his visitors.

"Few outsiders know of it," he signed confidentially. "Fewer still have seen it. I was fortunate, as a young man . . . I will tell you."

As soon as custom allowed the next morning, the travelers were on their way. It was only beginning to grow light. Tall Bull was extremely anxious.

"Let us hurry!" he urged.

"Bull," said Running Otter firmly, "now is the time to remain calm. If we show our concern, these people, who are friends of the horned ones, will become suspicious. They will send a messenger to warn them."

Tall Bull did not reply.

"Besides," observed the tracker, "we must spare our horses. We need them."

"But we can steal more from the Horn People," Tall Bull insisted.

"True. But that takes a little time. And first we must get there, and on *these* horses."

They managed to achieve a pace that was acceptable, even though not pleasing, to all.

Suddenly the tracker chuckled.

"What is it?" snapped Tall Bull irritably.

"I just thought," mused Spotted Cat, "if we hurry too

fast we will get there first. They are only a day or two ahead of us."

The three looked at each other.

"Could we?" asked Tall Bull. "An ambush?"

There was a quick discussion.

"No!" said Running Otter finally. "No, it is too dangerous. Three do not attack fourteen, even from ambush."

"But the surprise," pleaded Tall Bull. "That will help."

Spotted Cat spoke gently to him again.

"Tall Bull, we understand your need to fight, and that time will come. But not now. They will be alert, and would probably kill the girl if they are attacked."

"It is true, Bull," added Running Otter. "And we must know more about the place and its spirit. There is time."

"How do we know that?" demanded Tall Bull.

"Because the old man, the grower back there, told us. The ceremony takes four days, and they must prepare for it first. That gives us time to seek out the best plan, to steal horses, find our way around."

"We cannot go in."

"True. We will camp at a distance, and let Cat go in. He can make himself invisible."

The tracker grinned appreciatively. It was not true. Some holy men might, but he had never claimed to do so.

"Not really," he said modestly. "But there are tricks to play in the heads of others."

Tall Bull had heard all his life of the abilities of Spotted Cat. This man's reputation in the band was great.

"It is good, Uncle," he said respectfully. "And my heart is good, to have your help in this."

"Come, then, we travel," said Running Otter.

• • • •

A few days later, they lay on a hill overlooking the river. A haze of smoke hung over the town, partially obscuring the shapes of the domed earth-lodges.

"But where are the lodges?" asked Tall Bull.

"There . . . see the smoke coming out of the little hills?" Cat pointed carefully.

"Those? The mounds? They live inside?"

"It must be so. They do not move them as we do," Otter said.

"I know, but . . . *aiee,* in the *ground?*" Tall Bull felt a chill of dread at the thought.

"They have horses." Spotted Cat nodded toward a sizeable herd downstream. "I will look closer at them, see how best to steal."

"It is good," agreed Otter. "Now, let us make camp here, in the gully behind us. No fires. Cat will go and see what he can find."

"It is good," agreed the tracker. He glanced at the sun. "Let us camp. Then I will go down at sunset. Twilight is a good time to become invisible."

He smiled to himself at his little joke, and the three slid back out of sight before they rose to return to their horses, hidden in the brush below.

15

>> >> >>

Bear Paws saw his marriage continuing to erode away. They rarely spoke now, and love-making was a thing of the past. He knew that he was a large part of the problem, but did not know how to escape it.

The plight of the captive girl continued to worry him. He saw her nearly every day. At first he had tried to avoid coming too near, for fear she would recognize him as one of her People. Soon, however, he realized that there was no way that she could. His head was shaven, except for the horn-like tuft. His garments, his paint, all the customs he observed were those of the Horn People. And, what did it matter? The girl seemed to have no suspicion at all, of the gruesome climax to this ongoing event. Of course, none would tell her. She only knew that she was an honored prisoner. He had been a prisoner of these people, himself, before he became one of them. He had been treated harshly at first, but that was to be expected. After he was accepted, his treatment was good. Quite good, in fact. He could ask for no better. It had included the ecstasy of love. Pretty Sky . . . daughter of a prominent man in the clan. She had certainly saved his life by her wanting of him. Their romance had been exciting and bright, yet soft and warm, turning to thunder and lightning on occasion as they shared the marital bed.

Now, it was in ashes. He knew that it was only a matter of time until she chose another man to satisfy her needs. Among her people, it was her choice to do so. He would remain her husband, but . . . *aiee,* it was foreign to the way of his own people. How could he have thought that he could adapt to these strange customs? Of course, he had not known. Would he have entered this situation so readily, he wondered, had he understood the marriage customs of his wife's people?

But he had not understood. *Just as,* he thought, *the captive girl does not understand.* The outcome for her would be far worse, of course. He was suffering only the destruction of his marriage. The prisoner would lose her life itself. But meanwhile, she seemed to be enjoying her notoriety. Why would she not? She was pampered and fed, and dressed in the finest of buckskins.

The first day or two, it was almost an accident that he observed her in her outside exercise. After that, it was by design. He knew approximately when the women who were her guardians would bring her out, and he would plan to be there to watch. Only to watch. He had no other goal, no plan. He was only, perhaps, fulfilling a longing, a homesickness for the ways of his own, the People.

She was fair to look upon, in the flower of her maidenhood. There was beauty in her strong features, and the look of eagles shone in her eyes. Her body, tall and willowy, moved with an elegant grace.

He did not know her name. She was called by her title, the Morning Star Maiden. This bothered him. It was as if she were non-human, did not exist as her own person. In their eyes, he supposed, this was true. The bride of Morning Star *was* a supernatural being. She would become a deity when she crossed over. But the attitude of those who were her appointed guardians plainly said that she had already attained such status. She was already a deity. *Already dead,* he thought with a heavy heart.

Yet Bear Paws found himself unwilling to admit that this was inevitable, that the girl's future was hopeless. There must be something that he could do to rescue her. There was a little time to plan, because Hawk's Tail had not yet announced a time for the ceremony. Even after the old priest did so, there would be four days. *Four days,* while the girl still lived, to devise a plan for her rescue.

He spent much time alone, riding the surrounding country. It was easy to say that he hunted game, and he was believed. Actually, most of his time was spent in deep thought and planning. Rather, in trying to plan. Usually his schemes dissolved in fantasy before they even approached any real plan. His fantasies revolved around what would happen *after* the rescue. The grateful girl would fly into his arms, of course. They would spend days and nights of ecstasy while they traveled back to the People. There they would be welcomed in triumph and he would become a respected man of the tribe, to settle down with his grateful bride in a new lodge that would be their own.

Then he would shake his head to clear it of such dreams. It was ridiculous to think of such things. The girl did not even know he existed. Did not, in fact, know that her life was in danger. Then, there was also the reality that she was guarded at all times. Even if he did manage to reach her and inform her of the danger, how could they escape her guardians and break free? And after that, there would surely be pursuit. *Aiee,* it seemed hopeless.

Pulling himself back to reality, he finally realized that his only possibility was to learn as much as he could about the coming events. Red Hand was helpful, but there was a danger there, too. In his questioning, he must appear merely curious. If he showed too much interest, his friend would become suspicious. Then there was no way to tell how the man might react. A challenge to one's customs would not be taken lightly, even from a friend. So, he must take great pains to see that his friend suspected nothing. Red Hand had tried to kill him once, and would do it again if it seemed prudent.

Even so, he managed to learn much about the ceremony. The four critical days after the date was set would be occupied with rituals almost continually.

"Inside the lodge?" asked Bear Paws.

Red Hand paused, looking at him curiously.

"I mean, is the ceremony public?" Bear Paws explained clumsily.

"Partly inside, partly out. Some of it is public. Why?"

"I was only curious."

"Oh. Well, the last morning is public. Everyone will be there."

"Where?"

Again, Red Hand peered quizzically at his friend.

"Outside the town. The priest chooses the spot. Probably out there."

He nodded casually toward the east. This seemed a prudent time to change the subject, and Bear Paws began to talk of hunting and the weather, until they parted.

His hunts, almost daily, were timed carefully so that he could watch the Morning Star Maiden during her short time outside. Maybe he could see something, devise some plan born of desperation to help her. If he could only find a way to warn her and let her know that there was a friend who cared. But on the other hand, she was under the impression that she *was* among friends. Her guardians gave every indication of friendship and concern for her comfort and welfare.

Once more he came back to a hopeless conclusion, a trail that led nowhere. Nowhere, of course, except to the deadly ritual of Morning Star. He thought of shouting to her in her own tongue, warning of the danger. He should be able to get the idea across in only a few words, before any of the Horn People realized what he was doing. Then it would not matter what happened to him, as long as the girl was warned.

But it would, he knew. He would be instantly silenced, probably killed. He would be of little help to the prisoner if he were dead. And what use to her, to be warned, if her guardians knew of the warning? They would only tighten the security, restrain her if necessary, until that fateful morning when . . .

Adding to Bear Paws' problem was the fact that each time he saw the girl, he was so obsessed with her beauty. His thoughts refused to behave rationally. He doubted that he *could* call out to her sensibly, even if that seemed a possible choice.

Maybe there was some way to communicate with her without attracting attention. Instead of shouting a warning . . . *Yes!* He could *sing* it! No one here knew the tongue of the People. He would say that he was using a ceremony of his own tribe to bring back pros-

perity. He would tell Red Hand that there was a chant
used for such purposes. He would use nonsense words
until the proper time, and then when the girl was
brought outside he would start a chant that would
mean something to her but to no other. He began to
think of the words he would use.

"Listen to me, little sister, I come to help you . . .
You are in great danger . . . I come from the People,
our People, to help you . . ."

If he could do that, establish communication, he
could tell her more, tell her what plan he was devising
to free her. Of course he had no plan, but surely one
would come.

He must, of course, be careful not to alarm the prisoner so that she revealed the attempt to communicate.
Maybe at first merely one of the prayer chants which
she would know. A chant for the return of the Sun, the
grass, and the buffalo, perhaps. Then when she seemed
to recognize her own language (he would watch closely
for this), he would caution her to show no sign, while he
continued to inform her. Yes, that would be good.

His first step was to inform Red Hand of his intention
to perform a ritual of the People. Red Hand, of course,
was dubious.

"Why?" he asked.

"It may be of help. It is a part of the ceremonies of my
People, to bring back Sun and grass and buffalo."

Red Hand shrugged.

"Sun is already coming back. It is not time yet for
grass and buffalo. Besides, the Morning Star will do
this."

"Yes, I know," Bear Paws pushed on. "But this may
help, too. I want to help."

It was plain that Red Hand disapproved, but he said
nothing.

Bear Paws began that evening at sunset, chanting nonsense and keeping his own cadence on a small drum. The ceremony attracted little attention. He was an outsider, though he had adapted well. It was apparent that no one thought it unusual for him to perform a ceremony of his own tribe.

Yes, this would work, he thought triumphantly. Tomorrow, when the girl was brought outside, he would begin. Nonsense words first, then the Sun chant, until he could catch her attention.

He sat atop the earth-lodge, waiting. People looked at him casually, but seemed to see nothing amiss. He tried not to look toward the Morning Star lodge, yet kept it in view from the corner of his eye. His palms were damp, his every muscle tense.

There was a hint of motion at the other lodge, and he deliberately turned away. He lifted the stick and gave a tentative tap on his drum. Then, a high-pitched singing tone, without meaning, merely to establish a chant.

"Ah-ee-ah! Wo-ha . . ."

He got no further. He was grasped roughly from behind, the drum stick wrenched from his grasp. Startled, he turned. Hawk's Tail stood over him, his eyes filled with a strange intense madness.

"You will be silent!" he hissed. "No one must interfere with Morning Star."

The old priest was panting with emotion and with the effort of his dash to prevent Bear Paws' chant.

"There will be no other ceremony," he stated flatly. "I will have you killed if you do this thing."

He whirled and walked away, tossing the drum stick aside as he did so. Bear Paws looked after him, helplessly. The Wolf-man came out of the Morning Star lodge and looked carefully around, then motioned to the women. With great deference they ushered the girl out into the sunlight to walk. She appeared more beautiful than ever today, and Bear Paws' heart sank to think that he had failed.

It was that same night that the announcement came. Tomorrow would begin the four-day ceremony that would culminate in the marriage of the maiden to Morning Star.

16

»» »» »»

"**Y**ou are crazy!" Pretty Sky shouted at him. "You have gone mad over that girl!"

"I have not," he insisted. But he knew that she was right, at least partly.

"You have not been the same since she came," Sky yelled. "What is the matter with you? You know this is our way!"

"No . . . it . . . I . . .," he stammered, but she went on.

"I see you watching her whenever they come outside. And now you do this stupid thing . . . to start to sing!" She threw up her hands in despair and consternation.

"It is a ceremony of my people," he said in defense, though not exactly true.

"And you might have been killed for doing it!" she ranted. "You interfered with the Morning Star Priest. He could have had you killed! Bear Paws, you have

changed. It is this girl. You think you have fallen in love
with her, and this makes you ignore me!"

Bear Paws took a deep breath.

"It is you who does not speak to me," he insisted
angrily, "since long before this girl came."

"You, too!" Sky snapped. "And yes, before that. Since
long before. You have not been the same since last
autumn."

That is true, he thought to himself. *Since the Morning
Star Vision was announced.*

That had been the start of the trouble between them.
Or was it even earlier? He thought so. The excitement
of their early relationship was not the same. It had
begun to fade, even before this strange Morning Star
ritual that now obsessed him. He had felt trapped, carried along by a series of events over which he had no
control. In his own way, he was as much a prisoner as
the unfortunate Morning Star Maiden.

Now, he had made an attempt to break away, to do
something that would interrupt the cycle. It was as
much for himself as for the maiden, he now thought.
And his effort had failed. It had been at best a feeble
effort, he realized as he considered the failure. Worse,
he had engendered the wrath of the priest, and now he
would be watched more closely.

The whole thing had brought to a crisis the problem
of his rapidly-deteriorating marriage. The wrath of
Pretty Sky had been apparent to the entire village, as
the quarrel was quite public. Now in its aftermath people shuffled away, half embarrassed but chuckling quietly. He knew that anyone who had not chanced to
overhear would have heard the entire story of the quarrel by evening, anyway.

It was almost an anticlimax, then, when the announcement came. The Morning Star ceremonies would begin on the following day.

Four days. *Aiee,* so short a lifetime ahead for the beautiful girl of his own people. Four full days, five nights. Five days from this moment she would lie dead, her life blood drained away in homage to the Morning Star. So short a time, and he had no plan at all to help her.

He imagined himself, years later, when he might have contact with some of the People. They would know of his time with the Horn People, and of the girl who was sacrificed. How could he answer the suspicions that they would have? In his mind he imagined their questions.

"Were you there when our maiden was killed by the Horn People?" they would ask.

And he tried to imagine his attempts to answer.

"But I could do nothing to help her!" he protested. "I tried . . ."

Then he realized that he had spoken aloud. He looked around, embarrassed. He was sitting on top of the lodge, and there were people nearby. Some of them looked at him curiously, and then turned away, embarrassed. He had spoken in his own tongue . . . At least, he thought so. Those who overheard would think that he was lamenting his marital problems, and be sorry for him.

He could not decide which of those problems was the greater, his own personal crisis or that of the captive girl. They had a tendency to blur together in his mind. He would worry about one for a time, then the other. Or both at once. Sometimes he would slip into the escape of fantasy in his thoughts, and the one would become the answer to the other. In his mind he would see himself rescuing the girl from the very moment of the sacrifice, and carrying her to safety. Then would begin an idyllic life of forever-happiness, back among their own people.

He might as well try such a thing, he thought in desperation. His life here was over, with his marriage destroyed. It was for Pretty Sky to say, of course, but she had all but announced it today. There was only the formality of asking him to move out of the lodge. It would be customary for the estranged husband to go back to the lodge of his mother, but here he had none.

The children, of course, belonged to her. He was responsible for their support, but after all, he himself had not even a home here, if Sky decided that their marriage was at an end. Probably no one would expect him to stay. He could do so, could remarry here if he chose, but the idea was not good for him. No, he decided, he should leave, go back to the Sacred Hills. There the spirits of the land were more familiar, and Morning Star was only a minor deity.

Pretty Sky had not yet asked him to move out, so he would wait. Probably that would not come until after the ceremony of the Morning Star. Four days. Maybe he could stand it until then.

There remained, of course, the doubt about whether he could tolerate attending the ceremony. Or, he thought, knowing that it was happening, even if he did not attend.

Bear Paws spent a miserable night, awake for most of it, tossing restlessly, trying to be careful not to touch Pretty Sky in the robes near him. He thought that she was awake too, but tried to be as quiet as he could. He had no desire for a confrontation at this time.

When it was near dawn, he arose and slipped outside. He must get away, alone where he could think clearly. Even as he did so, there was a grim irony in his action.

Getting away alone had not yet allowed clear thinking on the problems that confronted him. He smiled ruefully to himself.

At least, he thought, it would be better than lying in the darkness of the lodge, wide awake. He filled his lungs with the crisp air of the pre-dawn. It was good to be outside, in the open. Maybe that was part of the problem, he thought. It had been difficult to adapt to living in an earth-lodge at first . . . a hole in the ground, fit for snakes and burrowing rodents, but hardly for a man. Surely not for a man of the People. Theirs was the open air of the wide grassland, the practical adaptability of the skin-lodge. Maybe the close air of the earth-lodge, which always seemed stale to him, had affected his brain over the years. It was a thought. His hardest task in adapting to the ways of the Horn People had been this. He still felt trapped sometimes as he stooped to enter. Trapped and enclosed, like a buffalo trapped by hunters in a box canyon, without means of escape. He had found it necessary to fight down the feeling of panic that he felt at first. The animal smell of the living quarters, somehow like the odor of a mouse's nest or . . . a bear's den, maybe.

He breathed deeply again, to clear his lungs of the stale air as he moved away from the lodge. He must get away. This was not a day to be around the village. The first day of ceremonies leading to the climax. After this, only *three* days.

He must not think such thoughts. He picked up his saddle, his bow and quiver, and moved toward the horse herd to catch his mount, glancing to the east as he did so. His purpose was to see how long until daylight, but he stopped still in his tracks at the sight.

The very first paling of the dark eastern sky was beginning, the yellow-gray of the false dawn. That was what he had expected. But there was also another sight. He supposed that he had seen it many times, all his life. Yet he had never experienced this feeling. To the northeast, the Morning Star was just rising. Red and angry, and larger than he remembered, it seemed to crawl up over Earth's rim, to enter the world of humans. To some, to the Horn People, perhaps, the sight may have been beautiful, inspiring. To Bear Paws it was not so. Morning Star had become an evil, malevolent thing, foreboding and threatening. It would rise only three more times before the fateful day, the last dawn of life for the Morning Star Maiden. He shuddered and moved on.

By the time he had located his favorite horse and saddled it, most of the stars were paling before the coming appearance of Sun Boy's stronger light. Morning Star still hung there, a trifle higher now, a trifle more pale. Bear Paws had the uncomfortable feeling that even after it was no longer visible, it would still be there, watching. It would pass across the sky, invisible, to rise again tomorrow. And the next and the next, until . . .

He shook his head. He must not let such thoughts occupy him. Surely it must be possible to resist the influence of Morning Star. He felt not only trapped by circumstances now, but actually threatened by the strange spirit. It seemed like an enemy to him, a personality who was determined to destroy him. Was he going mad, as Sky had suggested, but in a different way? It did not matter, he supposed. If he *felt* this threat by Morning Star, it was real. It was as if . . . well, as if he were not only threatened, but challenged. The evil red deity was laughing at him, daring him to try to interfere.

But this morning's experience had done something

to him. He was still concerned, depressed, even. Yet there was a change. He was ready to fight. Even if it became hopeless, he would die proudly as a man of the People. What better cause? He could see himself as he battled the hopeless odds, and the words of the Death Song came to him:

> *The earth and the grass go*
> *on forever,*
> *But today is a good day*
> *to die.*

And the morning, four mornings hence, would be one that the Horn People would long remember. What better cause? He might not free the Morning Star Maiden, but if she died, he would die protecting her. Thus, he might still protect her on the Other Side.

He rode to the top of a low rise and pulled his horse to a stop. He lifted his bow to the northeast, pointing his extended left arm at the red-glowing orb which still glared in the graying sky.

"Morning Star," he hissed, *"you yet have to deal with me!"*

Bear Paws could have sworn that the star twinkled slightly, as if in amusement. Maybe he *was* going mad. His primary reaction, however, was anger.

"You know me as Bear Paws, an adopted prisoner of your Horn People," he shouted. *"Know me now by my true name, Strong Bow of the Elk-dog People."*

He deliberately turned his back in insult, and rode slowly away without looking back.

17
» » »

Bear Paws pulled his horse to a stop. Something was not right. He sat listening, looking around him. He may have been careless, because he had been deep in thought. More worry than thought, actually. Since his confrontation with Morning Star earlier in the day, he had been riding aimlessly, trying to devise the details of his plan to challenge the deity. He had been preoccupied, and had neglected to pay attention to the ordinary measures of observation that one would normally take.

He could not quite define it, this ill-at-ease feeling that now overcame him. Of one thing he was quite sure . . . Something was not as it should be. Quickly but methodically he swept his gaze around the area, and saw nothing amiss. A red-tailed hawk circled high above, and its mate perched on the tip of a dead snag near the river. Closer at hand, birds sang undisturbed. On a far ridge, a coyote trotted lazily, carrying its tail at just the right sloping angle. This indicated no threat in that area. He watched three crows for a little while, because they are among the first of creatures to notice things that should not be, and sound the alarm. These crows were flying back and forth between two dead trees. After a little while, he decided that they were merely engaged in some game of their own. He smiled. Crows do such things.

He felt better, however, when a lone heron rose from somewhere on the river. Its course took the bird near the play area of the crows, but it did not waver. The dignified old heron would not divert from its purpose merely because of silly games of a group of crows. If there had been danger, it would have swung wide. This reinforced Bear Paws' impression, and he was reassured.

Maybe he had been mistaken. His whole being was so finely tuned, so alert . . . Yes, he must be overreacting, somehow. It was good that this had happened, to steady him, to place things in proper perspective. He lifted the reins and started to turn his horse.

The action was interrupted by a sound. It was muffled and distorted, but he had heard that sound many times, and instantly realized its significance. It was the snort of a horse. Not merely that sound, but such a snort, modified by a thong around the muzzle. There were many times, in unfamiliar territory or in the stalking portion of a hunt, when a horse *must not* cry out. In such situations, the loud whinnying call of the horse could be prevented. The trumpeting whinny requires that the mouth be open. If it is tied shut, the animal is limited to a soft snort.

Without even thinking about it, Bear Paws swung down and placed a hand around his own horse's nose. He pulled a thong from the bag at his waist . . . one always carried such things . . . and muzzled his own horse. Quickly he led it to a clump of dogwood and tied it, to remain concealed while he investigated.

He was certain that no other hunters from the village were in the area. The country was open, and even in his aimless circuit of the morning, he would have noticed other hunters. If this were true, then, whoever had muzzled the horse was an outsider. It seemed highly unlikely that an outsider would hunt in the territory of the Horn People, who were known for their ferocity.

The rider of the muzzled horse whose snort he had heard, then, must be an enemy. And he meant no good to the village. The quieting of the unseen horse was to conceal its presence and that of the rider.

There was a brushy ravine just to his left, and Bear Paws moved toward it, crouching low to avoid detection. His skin crawled at what might lie ahead. He could, of course, return to the village and give the alarm, bring more warriors.

But what could he report? That he was out riding around, and heard a horse snort? His credibility was already at low ebb. They probably would not even believe him. They were so concerned with their cursed ceremony. No, he must know more.

His nostrils caught an unmistakable whiff of familiar odor . . . smoke. *Aiee!* The man or men who were here had actually established a camp. They must be skillful, for there was no visible smoke whatever. The builder of this fire knew how to choose his fuel to avoid the telltale plume.

He flattened himself to the grass and wriggled forward on his belly. He now had an idea where the camp must be. In that brush-filled ravine ahead . . . there was no other place that such a camp could be concealed. He was approaching from the steep side, and would be able to look down into the camp. Very slowly and carefully he approached the rim, waited a little while, and then ventured to peer over into the pocket. The smell of the smokeless campfire was strong in his nostrils now.

A little clearing lay below, and a tiny fire burned in its center. A young man was seated on a rock, his back to the observer, and a few items lay around the area: sleeping robes, the weapons of the young man . . .

Something warned him, a sound, maybe, and Bear Paws started to turn. He was barely able to meet the rush of his assailant, to grasp the wrist of the hand that held the knife and deflect it. Even so, it was a close call, gashing a rent in the left shoulder of his buckskin shirt. He did not even notice, because he was fighting for his life. He had been duped, distracted by the presence of the man below, a decoy to catch his attention while the other performed the ambush.

The attacker was strong, a big man, well coordinated. They rolled back and forth in the narrow confines of space between the bushes, scratching and clawing, trying to knee each other's groin. Bear Paws could not draw his knife, because his hands were occupied in holding the knife-hand of the intruder. He saw the point waver, sometimes perilously close to his face. He must not weaken. For a few moments they struggled, neither able to dominate. The attacker seemed surprised at the strength in his intended victim. They were fairly evenly matched. This was a surprise to Bear Paws, too. Among his own people, he had been Strong Bow, noted for the strength of his arms and shoulders.

"Son of a snake!" the knife-wielder hissed at him. The man's face was close, the hate and anger that burned in his eyes frightening. The man's left hand clawed at his throat.

Then it occurred to Bear Paws, a surprise that almost made him lose his grasp on the flailing wrist. He had *understood* the insult. It had been in his own tongue. Not that of the Horn People, but his *own,* the language of the Elk-dog People of the Sacred Hills. This man was one of his own nation.

"Wait, wait!" he cried. "Stop! We are not enemies. We are brothers!"

He saw confusion on the face of his assailant. The firm grasp at his throat weakened only a little. In a moment, the man spoke, still panting from exertion.

"How are you called?"

"Bear . . . no, Strong Bow . . . Southern band . . ." he panted.

The other man seemed unconvinced.

"My brother is Red Horse, the holy man," Bear Paws panted.

"But you . . . a Horn-man!"

"I was their prisoner. Put your knife aside . . . we talk."

He was finding it a little hard to talk. The choking grasp on his throat had left him breathless.

"It is good you are here," he said carefully. "One of our women is in danger."

There was a momentary look of confusion on the face of the other man.

"Your women?"

"No. *Ours.* A woman of the People!"

The other man flipped the knife aside, though not too far.

"Now, let go my hand."

Bear Paws did so, and the two sat up, both still wary.

"How are you called?" Bear Paws asked, massaging his sore throat.

"I am Running Otter. Northern band. I have heard of your brother."

Now another man approached, ax in hand, ready for action.

"No," cautioned Running Otter. "He is one of us."

Bear Paws thought he recognized this as the man by the fire.

"Ah-koh," he greeted the astonished young warrior.

"This is Tall Bull," Otter introduced. Then he gestured toward his erstwhile opponent. "Strong Bow, of the Southern band." He was still panting from the exertion.

"How many are you?" Bear Paws demanded.

"Three . . . our tracker is out scouting your . . . the Horn People's village."

"Only three? Are there more nearby?"

"No. We follow the girl. She is my sister."

"And my wife-to-be," stated Tall Bull.

"Aiee! And you followed to help her?" Bear Paws asked.

"Yes. We have been told of the danger, by some growers." He jerked a thumb back in a southerly direction.

"Yes, it is bad," admitted Bear Paws. "I have tried to form a plan."

"You have seen her, then?"

"Of course. She is well . . . she knows nothing of the ceremony."

"Ah! We wondered about that. You have talked to her?"

"No, no. She is carefully guarded. I tried to sing to her."

"Sing?"

"Yes. In our tongue, to warn her. Their holy man stopped me."

"What can we do, then?" asked Tall Bull.

"I do not know, yet," admitted Bear Paws, "but now we are four. I was alone, there!"

The others nodded soberly.

"Oh, we must plan quickly," Bear Paws added. "They have a four-day ceremony, and it started today."

"*Aiee!* We had heard of the four days, from the growers. It is now?"

"Yes. This is the first day."

"Is she ever outside? Spotted Cat says she is kept in a hole in the ground."

Bear Paws smiled.

"Yes, their earth-lodges are so."

"You live so?" Tall Bull's look of disbelief was apparent.

"I have done many things that I . . . but let us plan."

Quickly, he told them of the daily routine, the way the village was laid out. It was good to talk to his own people, even under such circumstances.

"Let me think on this," he finished. "I will learn all I can of the ceremonies, and we will choose our time."

The others nodded.

"I will come here again tomorrow," he promised.

"Can you do that?"

"Yes . . . I have ridden out nearly every day. They are too concerned with their ceremony to notice."

"Spotted Cat says that one rides out," Otter said. "We thought it was one of their wolves."

"He saw me," admitted Bear Paws, a bit embarrassed. He should have been aware that he was watched.

"If you cannot come here," suggested Otter, "just ride out somewhere and wait. Cat will come to you."

"It is good!"

They parted, and Bear Paws turned back toward his

horse. He felt good, better than for many moons. It had been a good day, even though he had nearly been killed.

He untied his horse and removed the thong from its muzzle. The animal whinnied softly as he mounted to return to the village. He could actually see some hope, now. He was not able to see how he personally could escape, but it was entirely possible to free the girl, with the help that he now had. He had no plan yet. It would be necessary to learn more about the ceremony before he could do that.

But all in all, his heart was good. His life here among the Horn People was all but shattered anyway. This would be a good way to be remembered by both the Horn People and by his own. He would do whatever he must. It increasingly appeared that four mornings from now, it would be a good day to die, to go down fighting for one of his own, the Death Song on his lips.

But he must plan carefully, not to arouse suspicion. He looked at his dirty and torn buckskins, and the bloody gash across his left shoulder from Otter's knife. He must have a story. A fall from his horse, perhaps. Yes . . . the animal had shied from a real-snake, and threw him among the rocks. That would explain his appearance.

18

>> >> >>

There was a sacred fire burning in the Morning Star lodge now, Red Hand told him. It was lighted on the first ceremonial morning. Four long poles, of different kinds of wood: cedar, elm, cottonwood, and willow. It was a star-shaped fire, each pole representing a direction. As they burned, they would be advanced into the fire. This would allow the fire to burn throughout the four days of ceremony.

Each day there were private ceremonial rituals inside the lodge, and then more outside, for all to watch. Each day the Morning Star Maiden wore a different dress, the colors symbolic of the four winds.

Bear Paws tried not to ask too many questions. Not too few, either, because if he showed no interest at all, it would be apparent that his attitude was wrong. He decided to follow along with the crowd, to show as much interest as the others in the village, but no more. At least, no more than an outsider might, seeing the

Morning Star Ceremonies for the first time. Beyond that, he would rely on Red Hand.

His friend seemed to have moved past the reluctance to discuss the ceremonial preparations. Once it was out in the open, and Bear Paws knew the truth, Red Hand relaxed. It did not seem to have affected their friendship, and in fact Red Hand seemed willing to tell all that he knew of the ritual.

To an extent, Bear Paws felt that Red Hand was being kind because of his friend's marital problems. The entire village was aware, of course. There had been a number of spectators at the scene of the marital quarrel. In a short while, every living soul was aware that Pretty Sky had quarreled with her husband, the outsider. This would have probably been their most important subject for discussion, had it not been for the Morning Star preparations. It was obvious that the marriage was nearing its end. There had been a woman or two, even, who had gone so far as to flirt with him.

"They are making you know of their interest, in case you become available," Red Hand told him, half teasing.

"No, that cannot be," he protested.

"Yes," insisted his friend. "Look at them . . . a little older, in need of a man. You are strong, and not too ugly, though you do look like the plains people. There will be those who wish to bed with you."

Bear Paws saw the mischievous twinkle in his friend's eyes, and smiled ruefully.

"Maybe so. But I am not ready . . ."

Red Hand became serious.

"I know, my friend. My heart is heavy for you and for the trouble in your lodge."

In your lodge . . . there had been a time when those words brought thoughts that were warm and comforting. Now, he found himself avoiding the lodge, because it was a place that had become cold and impersonal. It had never been very private, living with the extended family of his wife's parents. But, the structure was large, and he had been treated well. After the first days of his captivity, at least. Sky's father, Lone Elk, was probably responsible for having protected his life at the time of his capture.

Elk was still civil to him, though not talkative. Kills-Three, Sky's mother, took an attitude much like that of Sky, turning her face away as if he did not exist. Only the children chattered happily to him, barely understanding that something was wrong about Bear Paws. Possibly they missed it entirely, he thought, with all the excitement of the ceremonies in progress.

He watched the next day, as the maiden emerged from the Morning Star lodge to go through the ritual. Her buckskins were resplendent, her hair brushed and shining, her face aglow with excitement. Old Hawk's Tail performed the dance steps and the chants, and the girl and her attendants retreated once more into the lodge.

The crowd began to drift away. Part of them seemed to be moving out of the village, to the east, and Bear Paws followed along. On a rise, about two bow-shots away from the village, some sort of construction was proceeding. This, too, seemed to be a sort of ritual.

Two heavy cottonwood posts were set in the ground, about two paces apart. Tied firmly between them was a pole, lashed with rawhide to the uprights at about knee-high. It was painted white, and decorated with feathers and white ears of corn. Directly below the cross-pole was a shallow pit.

Bear Paws looked around, puzzled. Two of the priest's assistants were bringing another pole. They

held it in place, about waist-high, while it, too, was
lashed to the uprights. Hawk's Tail was chanting as the
bindings were secured, and now fastened corn . . .
yellow, Bear Paws noticed . . . to the new pole.

"Tell me of this," he whispered to Red Hand, who
had joined him.

"This is the ladder," his friend explained. "One cross-
pole is added each day. You missed yesterday's. Each is
of different wood, for the four directions . . . like the
fire I told you of."

Bear Paws nodded.

"It repeats the journey of Morning Star as he sought
the marriage bed of Evening Star," Red Hand went on.
"There were four fierce animals that he had to kill, one
in each direction . . . one each day: Bear, Lion, Wolf,
and Bobcat."

"So . . . four directions, four animals, four days?"

"Yes."

"What is the pit below?"

"That," said Red Hand seriously, "is the marriage
bed."

Bear Paws did not answer, but his heart sank. Somehow, the entire sequence had seemed unreal until now.
Now, he had *seen* it. The "ladder" to the sky, to join
Morning Star in the nuptial ceremony. Two poles were
already in place . . . two more . . . *two days* left, before the fateful morning.

As soon as he felt that he could, he hurried away, to
tell the other conspirators what he had learned. He left
the village in the wrong direction, circled far upstream,
and finally came to the hidden gully.

He was startled as Spotted Cat appeared before him
suddenly. The man seemed to rise out of the ground.

"*Aiee!*" Bear Paws said softly. "You startled me! You
are the tracker?"

It was more an acknowledgment than a question.

"Yes. Spotted Cat. You are Strong Bow. Come."

The tracker led the way to the others, who waited, out of sight. They nodded a greeting as Bear Paws dismounted.

"What have you learned?" asked Tall Bull eagerly.

"I am learning more of the ceremony," he began. "I am made to think that the last morning is best for our plan."

"*Aiee!*" cried Tall Bull. "Is this not dangerous, to wait?"

Otter waved a hand to silence him. "It is already dangerous, Bull. Now let him talk."

"They are building a ladder, east of the village," Bear Paws continued. "It is there that it takes place."

Spotted Cat nodded. "I have seen this."

"There are poles to be tied across this ladder, one each day . . . the second today. The place has a little ravine behind it, with trees and bushes." He turned to the tracker. "You saw it, too?"

"Yes, I hid there. It is good."

"That will be better, easier than trying to free her in the village."

Spotted Cat nodded. "Yes."

Bear Paws turned to him again.

"Can horses be hidden there?"

"Yes. I will choose a place."

"Good. Now there are other things we must learn. I will come again tomorrow."

"Not here," suggested Spotted Cat. "It is better to meet in a different place each day."

Bear Paws was agreeable.

"Where?"

"Downstream. A bend in the river, where herons build their lodges . . . big trees?"

"Yes, I know the place. I will come."

"Wait, Strong Bow," said Otter.

He turned and drew out two fat rabbits which he handed to the visitor.

"A gift?"

"No," chuckled Otter. "An excuse. You have been hunting, no? This helps your story."

Bear Paws took the rabbits and swung into the saddle.

"It is good!"

The ride home *was* good. He felt excited, ready for anything now. It was, perhaps, a ridiculous way to feel. The situation was still grim, though no longer hopeless. They would make a valiant attempt at rescue, and his feeling for that was increasingly good. There was no way that the Horn People could suspect trouble, if he remained cautious. Spotted Cat apparently intended to do all of the scouting himself, and he appeared as capable as Otter had said.

Bear Paws had almost forgotten his own feeling of romantic attraction for the girl . . . Calling Bird, they had told him. When he had learned of her intended husband, his own ideas of romance had begun to fade. His entire attitude was changing. There had been a time when he was certain that he could not save the girl. He had meant to try, but feared that both would die in the attempt. That, he had been ready to accept. If it happened, he would cross over with her, to help her meet whatever faced them on the Other Side.

Now, with a hope of success, however slim it might be, his spirits soared. If they could bring a plan into reality, and save the life of Calling Bird, it would be a great day for the People. He knew that it was unlikely that they could all survive the attempt. He also knew that whatever details they devised for their plan, his would be the most dangerous part. He was already in the midst of the enemy, and knew of the skill of their warriors. He was willing to take that part, and the risks it carried.

In effect, Bear Paws had already given himself up for dead. He now wanted to speak well for the bravery of the People. It would fall to him to fight the delaying action while the others made their escape with the girl. He had no qualms about that. They would carry the story of his bravery back to the People, and there would be songs and stories of it for generations.

It was a way, he began to think, to solve his other problem, too. He would be spared the indignity of being rejected by his wife. Pretty Sky surely intended to announce the divorce shortly after the Morning Star Ceremony. It would never happen, because he would be gone. There was, after all, a slim chance that he would escape, and thus avoid the indignity of Sky's announcement. He would also escape the attentions of the various aging women who might want him, as Red Hand had said.

More likely, he would die fighting. That, too, he could accept. Since his marriage was gone anyway, what difference did it make? He had abandoned his family once, when he left the People. Now he was about to leave his wife and children, partly against his will. By dying, he would do them a favor. He would be not only paying his debt to his parents and to the People, but to Sky and the children. She would be able to mourn him for the appropriate time, and then seek a new husband. She would not even have to announce the divorce.

Meanwhile, he would have crossed over, satisfied that he had beaten Morning Star. He could imagine himself encountering that deity face to face. He would spit in the glowing red eye, and whatever might happen after that, he would know that he had won. And it would be good.

19
»» »» »»

"**D**o you think he can be trusted?" asked Tall Bull.

It was disturbing to the young man that the others hesitated a moment before answering. He was restless with the inactivity, and with his concern for the well-being of Calling Bird. Otter had tried to talk with him of this, to hold him in check.

"But I want to do something," protested Tall Bull. "We sit and do nothing, here."

"No," Otter reminded gently. "We must find how things are, first. Cat is doing that."

"Could we not ride in, kill those who hold her, and ride out?" insisted Tall Bull.

Otter chuckled quietly. "And be killed ourselves, leaving no one to help her?" He was quiet for a moment, and when Tall Bull did not answer, he continued. "It may come to that, but we cannot do it blindly. Let us learn all we can, and then we must have a plan."

That conversation had been before the coming of the stranger, who looked like a Horn-man but professed to be one of the People.

"Can he be trusted?" repeated Tall Bull.

"We must trust him, Bull," said Running Otter finally. "He can tell us of things even Spotted Cat cannot find out for us."

"But what if he lied, only to keep you from killing him? Maybe he has told the others, and they are laughing at us, waiting for him to bring us to where they can kill us!"

"That could be, maybe," admitted Otter. "But, he did come back. He has told us much."

Now the tracker spoke for the first time.

"I am made to think he speaks truth, Tall Bull. All I have seen is as he says. They build the ladder, as he told us."

"But he looks like one of the Horn People," protested the young man.

"And so would you," teased Spotted Cat, "if we shaved your head and drew your hair into a horn. A little face-paint . . ."

Then he looked at Running Otter, and understanding flowed between them for a moment.

"Do you think . . . ?" Otter asked.

"Maybe . . . it will be just before dawn. We must think on this, Otter!"

"Shave our heads?" asked Tall Bull.

"Yes . . . we might go unnoticed," mused Running Otter. "It would give us an advantage."

"But there is risk here," Cat pointed out. "If we all look like the enemy, we might kill each other by mistake."

"Strong Bow already risks this," Running Otter observed. "I have considered, too, the risks he takes to come here, even. We can do no less."

"Unless he plans only to trap us," reminded Tall Bull.

"No, I am made to trust him," Spotted Cat answered. "If he wished to kill us, he could have returned with a war party, and we would be dead already. No, I have watched him. He moves in secret, and goes to much trouble to do so."

"Let us speak more of this other," Otter said. "What do you think, Cat? Of the head-shaving . . . ?"

"We must think more on it," answered the practical tracker. "If we do, we should have some way to recognize each other in a fight."

"Can we not call out to each other?" asked Tall Bull.

"Sometimes. But you have not been in a fight, Bull. Things happen fast. There is no time to ask questions. You shoot first . . . there is always danger of shooting each other, even in the best conditions."

"Well," observed Running Otter, "if we trust Strong Bow, we must trust him all the way. Let us see what he says about the head-shaving."

"Wait," said Tall Bull. "If we use some way to recognize each other, and tell him, then we will be marked if he does want to betray us."

"Aiee!" exclaimed Otter. "If he does, we are all dead anyway, Bull. My sister, too. But I think we must trust the man. He is our best hope. Remember, he could have had us killed by now if he wished. Besides, if he is loyal to the Horn People, he will not want to interrupt their ceremony just to kill some outsiders."

"That is true," agreed Cat. "The ceremony is too important to them. It would not be disturbed to ambush us. No, his heart is good."

The tracker rose and prepared to leave the little camp. Shadows were growing long.

"I go to watch them," he announced, though his intentions were obvious. "I will see if the ladder progresses as he says. Maybe I can see more of how the men shave their heads around the sides and leave that knot on the top."

The others chuckled, and the tracker faded into the twilight.

"Why do you wish to know all these things?" asked Red Hand, as they watched the next step in construction of the ladder.

Bear Paws hesitated a moment. He must be very cautious, now, not to arouse suspicion.

"I do not know, my friend," he answered carefully. "It is so foreign to my people . . . I am curious, I suppose."

"It is distasteful to you?" Red Hand asked probingly.

"Of course." He paused a moment, thinking. "To you, too, maybe? You hinted that when we first talked of it."

Red Hand now paused before answering.

"Maybe," he said finally. "But it is our way. You have told me that your people do not eat bears, but some of your allies do."

"That is true. Our sister nation, the Head Splitters, eat bear meat, and we do not."

"Yes. This is much the same. This is our greatest festival, as important as your Sun Dance."

"You know of our Sun Dance?"

Red Hand shrugged. "All the hunting nations have a Sun Dance, do they not? The Lakotas, north of us . . . Besides, you once mentioned it."

Both men chuckled, Bear Paws a little nervously. He wanted to argue that this was different, a greater concern than eating bear meat or holding the Sun Dance.

As sacred as the Sun Dance might be, it did not involve the taking of a life. And a girl . . . a maiden in the flower of her womanhood. *Aiee* . . . But he said nothing.

"You do not understand this, as I would not understand your Sun Dance," Red Hand suggested.

A thought came to Bear Paws.

"It is true," he agreed quickly. "And, if you were among my people, you would ask, to learn. I do the same." This, he hoped, would furnish an explanation for his questions. "It is good to know," he went on. "I have tried to learn the customs of my wife's people."

There. That should distract Red Hand's suspicions. He would be thinking more of the failed marriage than of the ceremony, and his friend's curiosity concerning it. Bear Paws saw the sidelong glance, a pitying look that told of sorrow for the marital failure. Good. Where there was pity there would be less suspicion.

He had gone to great lengths to avoid such suspicion. It was no problem at home. There was a strong impression that his absence was something of a relief to Pretty Sky. She must feel sadness, too, at the loss of what they had had. It would be hard to tell him that it was over. An odd thought . . . but no matter, it would soon be over. Sky would be relieved of the burden of her unhappy marriage to an outsider.

Actually, it was working to his advantage. His daily absences were welcomed, rather than suspected. It allowed him far more freedom of movement. Odd, he reflected, how when things are going well, each part seems to fit. This must be a good omen. Then he smiled to himself at such an interpretation. He must remember to ask his brother the holy man about that. Surely the thought had occurred to such a thinker as he.

Now Red Hand pointed to the scaffold. The assistants

of the Morning Star Priest were carrying the third of the poles to be fastened to the uprights. This, of yet a different wood, was painted and decorated with red, and that was the color of the symbolic ears of corn to be fastened at the ends.

It appeared more difficult to fasten this pole in place. It would be shoulder-high, and must be held at that level while the rawhide lashings were placed.

One more, thought Bear Paws. *One more day to devise the plan.* The plan was forming in his mind now, but it would depend on the timing of the ceremony. He must learn all he could of that, and quickly.

"You will attend the ceremony?" Red Hand asked.

Good, he thought. This would allow him to ask questions.

"Of course," he answered aloud. "But you must tell me of the meaning of these things."

Red Hand nodded. "It will be so. You know of this part."

"Yes. But of the ceremony itself."

"Later. I will explain as it happens."

No! Bear Paws thought in a panic. *I must know already, to plan and tell the others.*

"It is good," he said aloud.

He must not be too demanding, but would ask questions, continuing to be careful. Tomorrow would bring about the final preparations, and he could ask more detail about everything . . . the last rung of the ladder as it went into place, the pit that had been described as the marriage bed.

For now, he must hurry to meet the tracker and the others if they, too, came to the meeting place. Spotted Cat would be the important one in stationing the others in their proper places. He knew the terrain. Bear Paws had the strong impression that this man had been all around, probably *into* the village itself. He was most skilled at his special gifts. It was said, the others had told him, that Spotted Cat could become invisible. It was good. They could use every advantage in the coming dawn. Invisibility might not be actually possible, but the reputation alone told of great skill.

"I think I will hunt a little while," said Bear Paws as they walked back toward the village.

"It is good," agreed Red Hand. "I will go with you!"

No! Bear Paws wanted to cry out. *You must not!*

But he also must not arouse suspicion. How could he . . . *ah, yes!* The tracker would be waiting at the river bend. Bear Paws could lead the hunt near there, but not too near. Then it could be seen that he was unable to meet as planned.

At least, he hoped so. If Spotted Cat misunderstood, it would be bad indeed. But he must trust.

"It is good!" he answered. "Come, let us get our horses."

He could possibly get away later, though it seemed unlikely. Everything would depend on a single planning session tomorrow.

Tomorrow. For someone, perhaps many, the last day to live. It was a sobering thought. He must not meet with such a problem tomorrow when he rode out. Somehow, at all costs, he must avoid the companionship of Red Hand. Yet he must be with him enough to find out about the ceremony, and to make his plans.

Their hunt was a failure, yet a success for the purpose of Bear Paws. He was certain, when they skirted the bend where the herons nested, that somewhere Spotted Cat was watching, and would understand his predicament.

His faith was justified that night, as he made his way

out of the village a little way to relieve his bladder before retiring. A dark form rose in front of him.

"Strong Bow!"

It was not a question, but a greeting.

"Spotted Cat?"

"Yes."

"I could not come . . ."

"Yes, we know. Tomorrow, same place?"

"It is good. Cat, I . . ."

There was a sound of someone coming, and the tracker faded into the darkness as if he had never been. Maybe he *was* invisible!

The other man nodded a greeting, and began to fumble with his breechclout.

"A nice night," he mumbled.

"Yes," agreed Bear Paws. "A little chilly."

20
»» »» »»

Bear Paws watched the fourth pole lifted into position and lashed there, completing the ladder. There was a finality about it, a sense once more that he had no control over any of these things that were happening. He must fight such feelings, he told himself. There must be no doubt in his mind that he *could* effect a change in the plans of the Morning Star priest.

Some will die, he thought, *but not the girl.* For some, this was the last day of life, and he wondered who. Anything might happen when the time came for action. Well, so be it.

They were lashing a fifth pole to the uprights now, well above the others. He turned to Red Hand.

"What is this?"

"That one is not part of it," his friend answered. "The girl stands on the top pole of the other four, and holds on by this one."

How can she be persuaded to do this? thought Bear

Paws. Surely, somewhere in the ceremony, the captive would realize that there must be a climax to all this honor. At what point would it come? And what could induce her to stand on the ladder while someone prepared to loose the Sacred Arrow at her heart?

As if in answer to the question that he had not voiced aloud, Red Hand spoke.

"She will be tied."

"Tied?"

He had not foreseen this. He had thought merely of calling to her to run, and then defending her retreat by stopping any pursuers.

"Yes . . . her wrists are tied to the top pole," Red Hand explained.

Bear Paws tried to conceal his shock. Somehow, the whole thing was still unreal. His mind had refused to look at the actual physical reality of the ceremony. Now it became real to him. He was standing here, looking at the pole to which those slender wrists would be tied. He could imagine the horror of the moment when the girl herself realized the intent of her captors. Would she scream, fight, and claw? It would be a difficult task to tie the victim high on that ladder unless she cooperated. It could be done, he supposed, by simple force of numbers. The priest had many assistants.

He noticed a couple of these assistants walking down the east side of the little knoll.

"Where are they going?" he asked.

"They will prepare a special fire," Red Hand explained. "It will be out of sight. There they prepare the Sacred Arrow in the morning."

"Not until then?"

"No . . . well, the arrow is ancient, handed down from the first holy man. It is kept in the Morning Star

Bundle. The priest takes it out and blesses and purifies it just before its use."

Bear Paws was not listening well. He was distracted by the grim facts of the account. But the next words of his friend drew all his attention instantly.

"The purifying happens after the bride is on the ladder."

After! In later thoughts, Bear Paws wondered whether his friend had intentionally emphasized this fact. Whether intentional or not, this was the most important information so far. *After* the girl was on the ladder, there would be a ceremony that would take the holy man and the Wolf-man away from her for a little while. Possibly the assistants, too. Would the girl be left unguarded? Surely not . . . he dared not ask, but the moment for action would surely come at that time. The plan, such as it was, could be aimed at that short space of time when the girl would be less closely guarded.

Bear Paws, with what he hoped would appear a logical degree of curiosity, wandered down the far side of the knoll. The assistants to the priest were preparing a place for a small fire, bringing fuel and tinder. It must be ready to light quickly, he assumed. One of the assistants glared at him, seemingly in disapproval, and Bear Paws retreated.

He had seen what he needed, the location of the sacred fire. He had been concerned that it was too near the brushy draw where he hoped to hide the horses of the rescuers. But it was not so. Having satisfied himself of that fact, Bear Paws wandered casually back to the site of the ceremony. There were still a number of curious onlookers, and Red Hand was still among them.

"Did you see?" he asked.

"Yes. They are preparing a fire."

Red Hand chuckled. "It is as I said, no?"

Bear Paws nodded.

The poles were now secured, and the assistants, under the direction of the priest, had turned their attention to the shallow pit below. They had opened a pack that seemed to contain a mass of downy feathers. Breath feathers, the People would have called them, thought Bear Paws. The fluffy down from the breast of a goose or duck, of purest white, gathered from many birds, had been saved carefully for this most important of ceremonies. The men were spreading the soft material in the pit, smoothly and evenly, covering the entire area beneath the ladder.

"The marriage bed," said Bear Paws, half to himself.

"Yes," answered Red Hand. "There will be food placed there, too, for Morning Star. Dried meat, and the heart of a buffalo. They have already gotten that."

"Is it eaten?" Bear Paws asked.

He really did not care, but felt that he must keep up the pretense of curiosity. Red Hand looked at him strangely.

"Not here . . . in spirit, yes, so it is said. Here, it is anointed with the blood of the bride . . . part of the ceremony of crossing to the Spirit World."

It was difficult to maintain his composure, but Bear Paws managed to do so. He was eager now, to get away, to ride out and meet the others. At least, Spotted Cat. He was unsure whether the others would come or not.

As he saddled his horse, Bear Paws realized that this might be for the last time. It was good, though, that the subterfuge was nearly over. He was becoming fearful that someone might become suspicious of his daily rides. Well, no matter, this was the last of those. *The last day.*

He was glad that Red Hand said nothing about accompanying him today. Of course, Bear Paws had taken care *not* to mention such a ride. He could not conceal his intentions from his friend much longer. But he would not have to do so, now. For better or worse, it was nearly over.

He told no one when he rode out, but no one seemed to notice. His daily routine must have become so familiar that any observer would think nothing of it. Besides, there were more exciting things going on to distract the villagers.

He rode a long arc, heading first in the wrong direction, and pausing a little while to watch his back trail. It was critical, today, that he not be followed.

Finally he came to the bend of the stream where the herons made their lodges, and rode among the giant cottonwoods. Their buds were just beginning to burst into full leaf in the glory of the Moon of Awakening. Soon it would be the Moon of Greening . . .

Although he was expecting it, he was surprised when Spotted Cat appeared from a fringe of dogwood.

"*Ah-koh,*" the tracker said softly. "Come."

Bear Paws dismounted and muzzled his horse, then followed Spotted Cat into a denser part of the grove, where the others sat. He nodded in greeting.

"*Ah-koh,* my brothers. I could not come yesterday."

"Yes, we knew," said Running Otter. "It is nothing. What have you learned?"

"Ah, I have learned much," Bear Paws answered, squatting with the others. "I have learned more of the ceremony. *Aiee,* these Horn People have strange customs!"

Any chance onlooker would have been startled that such a remark would come from a man who appeared to be a warrior of the Horn People. Running Otter smiled at the thought. But it reminded him . . .

"Speaking of such," he began, "we have wondered if

we should shave our heads like yours, to be less easily noticed."

Bear Paws thought for a moment.

"I think not. The light will be poor. It would be harder not to kill each other."

The others nodded agreeably.

"While we speak of that," Bear Paws went on, "I hope you will take much care not to shoot *me*. I will look like one of the Horn People."

There was a short silence, and Running Otter finally spoke.

"Our brother, we have talked of this. We wondered at first whether you could be trusted. We decided so. You have helped us, and at danger to yourself. So, we are made to think that your heart is good."

Bear Paws was deeply touched.

"I . . . I must help my own . . ." he mumbled lamely.

Otter waved him down.

"Let me go on. Since we trust you with our lives, you must also trust us, no?"

"That is true," admitted Bear Paws.

"So, be sure that none of us will shoot you. Except by accident, of course."

Everyone chuckled at the grim joke.

It is good, thought Bear Paws, *to be among the People.* "It is good," he said aloud. "At least, I think so."

"Tell us, now," said Spotted Cat, "are you going home with us?"

Bear Paws was silent for a moment. He had failed to think beyond the rescue itself, he now realized. He had, in effect, as he shaped the plan in his mind, decided that he would be killed in the skirmish. But Spotted Cat was right. It is not good to plan for failure. If it happens, so be it, but it should not be planned.

"I had not thought of that yet, my brothers. But let it be so!"

The others nodded enthusiastically.

"It is good," said Cat. "I will steal a horse for you, too. You want your own, this one?"

There was quiet laughter.

"Yes, if you can," Bear Paws agreed.

"It is good. Leave your saddle where I can find it. And, I have already chosen the horse and saddle for Calling Bird."

"Good," said Bear Paws. This tracker was a remarkably skilled man. It was easy to see why Running Otter, as leader of the rescue party, had chosen him.

"You will want us with the horses in the little ravine?"

"Yes. Now let us plan. Here is what I have learned."

Rapidly, he described the ceremony as he understood it, with emphasis on the short while that would be critical to the rescue.

"I will be in the front row," he told them. "I will call out at the right time."

Tall Bull seemed concerned.

"Is it safe to wait so long?" he asked.

Running Otter laid a hand on his shoulder.

"Bull," he said, "I know that you have the hardest time of all. But think . . . is it safe *not* to wait? We must listen to our brother, here. Only he has the knowledge to say when is the moment."

"Tall Bull, I can understand, too," added Bear Paws. "It will not be easy for you. Let us talk of this. When Calling Bird realizes what is happening, she may cry out. But that is when you *must not* do anything. If you show yourself while they are tying her, with all the holy man's assistants there . . . *aiee*, not only you, but she, too, will be killed."

"That is true," agreed Otter. "If this is to be successful, you must do exactly as Strong Bow says."

"Yes, I am trusting you not to shoot me by mistake. You must trust me."

"It is good," said Tall Bull. "Now, what is my part?"

"Let us talk of the parts we all must do," said Bear Paws, who was now beginning to think of himself as Strong Bow. "We must have you three and the horses in the ravine well before dawn. I will come with the others, and will sit in front. Now, who is the best horseman?"

The three men looked at each other for a moment.

"Tall Bull," said Spotted Cat simply.

"That is true," agreed Running Otter.

"It is good. Bull, yours is the most important part of the plan."

Rapidly, Bear Paws told of his plan for the rescue.

"But that will leave you without defense," protested Otter.

"The surprise will help me," Bear Paws said. "And maybe, if Tall Bull does not need too much help, one of you could protect my back."

The others thought for a moment.

"It is dangerous, but I see no better plan," admitted Otter. "We will do our best to help you."

"My brothers," said Spotted Cat. "I am made to think that we can do this thing!"

21
» » »

Bear Paws lay in the darkness of the lodge, waiting for the time to come. He had not slept at all, during the long night which was to be his last in this lodge. He still felt that in all likelihood he would not survive the coming conflict.

He lay there with many regrets. He would have liked to say good-bye to Pretty Sky. There had been good times together, before they drifted apart. He had been unable to confide in her for many moons, and they had hardly spoken since their public quarrel. If it had been possible, he would have liked to try to explain how he felt. Maybe he could have made her understand. She would not even need to agree, if she could only see that for him it must be this way.

But, in the strange way that he had become entrapped in these events, it had now become impossible to talk to her at all. His primary mission in life, it now seemed, was to interrupt and destroy this ceremony, to free the captive girl and return her to her people. Look-ing back, it seemed that he had had no choice. For a long time, he had been headed toward this one event. It was a thing of purpose, a thing that he must do.

Pretty Sky would have understood, he thought, if he had the chance to explain it to her. He had been guided by outside forces into this action, as surely as Hunts-Well had been chosen by his Morning Star Vision to be Wolf-man. Yes, it was much the same, maybe. This was the vision, the call for Strong Bow of the People.

He wondered how far back this influence might have started. When Hunts-Well had his vision? When old Hawk's Tail announced that one was expected?

Or, did it begin long ago, when Strong Bow was cap-tured by the Horn People and became Bear Paws? Even before, maybe. What had made him defy his par-ents and the advice of his brother the holy man? It seemed so illogical, so childish now, that he had left his own people to join the ill-fated expedition of the Span-ish. Had *that* been part of his mission, too, to place him here for this purpose? Did his long and winding trail start then? Maybe, even, at his birth or before.

His heart was pounding with the excitement of it all. Yes, he was certain that there was purpose in his life, that this was to be the moment for which he was des-tined. He hoped that he would be allowed to talk of it with his brother, who was skilled in such things.

And, yes, he was sure that Pretty Sky would under-stand. Hers was a culture whose customs would lend themselves well to her beginning a new life. She could choose a new man, as was their way. No one would think anything of it, except, probably, that she had bet-tered herself. But he longed to feel that she would understand. There was no way for him to even hint at how he felt, without letting her know that he was leaving. That, of course, would risk the whole attempt at rescue.

No, she must not even suspect, until he was gone. If he were killed, or if he survived and merely went away with those of his own people. It would not matter, for Pretty Sky. Either way, she would be free to choose another husband. She should have no difficulty there. There was not only the prestige of her family, but her own beauty. Even with the trouble between them, he still admired that. There was probably no woman in the village nearly as beautiful as she. He had to admit that he still had strong feelings for her. That was why it would have been good to try to explain . . . But, no matter. It was something that, if he lived, would remain as a cherished memory.

And the children . . . *aiee,* that too would be a heartache. He had not been as close to the children as he wished, but that was the way of the Horn People. At least, he saw it so. Among his own, there was a closeness that to him seemed impossible among fathers and children with his wife's customs. Actually, it seemed that the most important man in a child's life here was usually the mother's brother. Pretty Sky had none, so her father, Lone Elk, had assumed a close relationship. He had great respect for Elk, a leader among his people. Elk would see to the raising of the children.

He mentally shook himself. He must not be thinking such thoughts. It would affect his performance in the morning, if he let such things bother him. No, he assured himself, Sky and the children would be well cared for, and he need not worry for them. He could worry for himself and for his loss later. For now he must think of the task at hand.

He forced himself to think of what must be happening at this moment. Spotted Cat and the others would be bringing the horses, carefully muzzled, to the little wooded ravine behind the knoll where the ladder stood. By this time they were probably there. Each of the three would have his own tasks . . . Tall Bull to be ready with the horse, for the right moment to act. One of the others, probably Otter, would keep the other horses in readiness. Spotted Cat must be alert and within close reach, to assist if anything should go wrong.

Bear Paws wondered what sort of a horse Cat would have stolen for the girl. He would choose well, no doubt. Cat would know her riding ability and would choose her mount accordingly. It would have to be sturdy, fast, and durable.

He wondered whether the tracker would be able to find his black stallion. He hoped so. It was a wonderful horse, and a prized trophy of war with the "Enemy" from the north.

Ah, he was thinking in terms of *after* the rescue, and that was good, he told himself. An omen for success! His spirits lifted.

It was a long time before dawn when the others in the lodge began to stir. Bear Paws went outside, and found that others, too, were stirring. There was an excitement in the air, a sense of anticipation in the predawn darkness.

People were beginning to drift in the direction of the ceremonial ladder. He must hurry, to find a place on the front row. He started to turn back, to call to those in the lodge to come on, but decided against it. It did not matter now. He hurried away.

Some were already seated, but he managed to find an appropriate place, directly in front of the ladder. The air was still, so still that it did not even stir the breath-feathers in the marriage bed below. It was starkly white in the dim starlight. People talked only in whispers, a murmur of quiet excitement in the darkness.

A night-bird called in the wooded ravine, and Bear Paws wondered if it was really a bird, or the rescue party, signaling to each other. Or, to him. Yes, they might be letting him know that all was well. That was probably it . . .

A dark form crowded in beside him, and sat.

"Ah, Bear Paws," said Red Hand.

Bear Paws had not counted on this. When the time came for action, what would his friend do? Try to stop him? If so, Red Hand could surely do it. His ax could be plainly seen at his waist, even in the dim light. Bear Paws himself was unarmed, except for a small flint knife.

He had pondered a long time about that. It was with a great deal of dread that he realized he could carry no weapons for defense. Both hands would be required to climb the scaffold and release the girl. The knife that he had chosen was ideal for slashing . . . for buckskin fetters . . . but virtually useless in a fight. Yet, he saw no other way. He had abandoned his bow in the lodge, regretting its loss.

The realization that Red Hand was wearing his ax led to another thought. Many of the men behind him would probably be carrying their weapons. He should have brought the bow . . . no, there would be no time to retrieve it, anyway. It was too late now . . .

There was a stir behind him, and he turned to see a procession coming out of the village, marked by the light of torches. In the lead was the Morning Star Priest, his arms and body painted strangely in black and white. Behind him was an assistant with a torch, which shed its flickering light on the main figure of the drama.

The girl walked serenely, proud and tall, stalking majestically up the slope toward the scaffold. She was flanked by two of the priest's assistants, also bearing torches. Behind her walked Hunts-Well, the Wolf-man. A last assistant brought up the rear with another torch. It was an impressive procession.

The spectators parted to let them pass. The priest, bearing his sacred bundle, passed within arm's length of the nervous Bear Paws. Then, naturally, so did the torch bearer and the maiden. He had never seen her so closely. She was dressed in a fine buckskin dress of black, and painted on her forehead was the sign of Morning Star. His skin prickled, and he gritted his teeth to keep himself quiet. The girl was beautiful, even more so at this close distance. She did not look right or left, but straight ahead, at the ceremonial ladder.

Bear Paws followed her gaze, and saw the angry red star, just crawling into view, between the uprights. Even in this moment, he realized the skill that must be required on the part of the Morning Star Priest, to make all this come together.

The girl turned and faced the crowd, and the priest began a solemn chant. Her face was still serene and proud. *She does not know!* thought Bear Paws. She turned, and began to climb the ladder, pausing at each step for the chant to change.

What has she been told? Bear Paws could not imagine that the girl was a willing participant.

Two of the assistants now placed their torches at either side of the ladder, apparently in sockets previously prepared. The two mounted the ladder to assist the maiden to the last step. Even now, she showed no concern, as she grasped the overhead pole. Had she been given a potion of some sort, he wondered, to dull her senses?

Each of the men on the ladder now produced a strap

of soft buckskin and looped it around a slender wrist, tying it loosely to the pole. Then they quickly descended, to take their positions beside the upright posts.

With much ceremony, the Morning Star Priest began to untie the sacred bundle, chanting all the while. Symbolically, he scattered a few more feathers of down into the pit. Then he deposited there a small packet of meat, and the buffalo heart that Red Hand had mentioned.

He straightened and reached again into the pack, to withdraw a short, stout bow and a red-painted arrow . . . *the Sacred Arrow!*

The moment was coming. Bear Paws gripped the haft of his knife. Now the priest turned away and followed one of the torch bearers toward the purification fire. The Wolf-man and another torch bearer followed, leaving the two still standing by the uprights.

Two of them! Bear Paws had not counted on this . . . he hoped that Spotted Cat was alert. He glanced at the face of the girl. Her expression had changed. She had realized now that she was betrayed. He expected a scream, but there was none. Without losing a particle of her dignity, the girl lifted her face and began to sing, chanting an improvised prayer.

"O, Great Spirit, save me from these people . . ."

The priest and the others were out of sight, now. It was time . . . it could wait no longer.

"Help is coming!" he shouted to the girl in her own tongue.

Then, hardly realizing it, he was running forward, voicing at the top of his lungs the full-throated war cry of the People.

Everyone sat for a moment in shocked silence. There was even the space of a heartbeat when he was able to hope devoutly that the others were in position when he had sounded the signal. If not, it was already over.

22

>> >> >>

Everything was happening at once, now. One of the men guarding the scaffold stepped forward to meet the rush of Bear Paws. He appeared confused, and hesitated a moment. Only a moment, but this and the force of the rush allowed Bear Paws to knee him in the groin. The man doubled over in pain and Bear Paws shoved him aside.

The other guard now overcame the surprise and stepped forward. Bear Paws stooped to grasp the torch at his feet and thrust it at the other's face. The guard turned aside, but the burning brand seared across the side of his head and neck. He cried out in pain.

This is taking too long! Bear Paws thought. *I will not be ready for Tall Bull.*

He climbed up the ladder, toward the confused girl. He could see the fear in her eyes, reflected in the flickering torchlight. He realized that she might think him an attacker. There was nothing about him to distinguish him from any other of the Horn People.

"I am of your people," he yelled at her. "I will cut you free. Tall Bull is coming with a horse!"

There was only an instant of confusion before she nodded in understanding. Meanwhile Bear Paws was slashing at the tough buckskin lashing on the girl's left wrist. He was forced to turn his back to slash the fetters, and the nape of his neck prickled with the knowledge that someone might strike him down at any moment. He must hurry.

The crowd was coming alive now. There were a few questioning shouts and some were rising to their feet. At first, apparently, many had thought that the rush of Bear Paws was a part of the ceremony. Unprepared for such an unexpected attack, they were slow to respond.

Even so he felt, rather than saw, the approach of several people. Someone grasped his ankle, and he kicked free. He wondered how many warriors had brought weapons to the ceremony, and the memory of the ax at Red Hand's waist crossed his mind. One blow to his unprotected legs and feet would quickly end the rescue attempt.

The buckskin thong parted, and the girl's left arm swung free. She pivoted to help him, and he started slashing at the other fetter.

"Look out!" she cried suddenly.

He turned to see a man with an ax mounting the scaffold. It was not Red Hand, and he was glad. But how was he to defend against this . . . ? Before he could act, the girl seized the upper pole with her free hand, and swung both feet. The length of her legs added to the force of the blow. Her moccasined feet struck the face of the attacker, and he tumbled backward off of the ladder to land with a loud thud below. He struck on the back of his head and shoulders and did not move. Bear Paws continued to slash at the tough leather strap. *Where is Tall Bull?*

As if in answer, a horseman burst from the trees and into the circle of torchlight. Tall Bull, roaring the People's war cry, kicked the animal forward, knocking aside men who were running toward the scaffold. He reined close, and as the leather lashing parted, freeing the girl's right hand, she was able to drop to the horse's back behind Tall Bull. He jerked the animal's head around, it pivoted neatly on its haunches, and they were gone into the night.

Bear Paws dropped to the ground on the other side of the ladder, for what protection it afforded.

"This way," shouted Spotted Cat. Bear Paws turned in that direction. A man darted around the upright and rushed at him. He turned to meet the attack, nearly defenseless with only his small knife. The man swung an ax at him and missed as Bear Paws dodged. Several others were crowding behind the man with the ax. There was a narrow gap between the upright post of the scaffold and a clump of sumac that formed a tight thicket. He realized that the ax man was standing in that space, and thus preventing the others from reaching him. Only then did recognition come.

"Red Hand!"

"Go!" hissed his friend, raising the ax again but withholding his swing until Bear Paws could dodge away again.

Another warrior slipped between the poles of the scaffold and struck at him with a club of some sort, striking his right shoulder. Bear Paws dropped his knife, and turned away, completely defenseless now.

But now the Morning Star Priest and the Wolf-man came running, followed by the other two torch bearers.

Bear Paws' heart sank. Hunts-Well, the Wolf-man, rushed at him, a crazed look of fury in his eyes. Old Hawk's Tail stood numbly, holding in his hands the sacred bow and arrow.

Bear Paws was never certain where Spotted Cat came from. He seemed to appear out of nowhere, as Bear Paws had seen him do before. How . . . ? But there was no time to even think of such things. In one swift motion the tracker snatched the red-painted arrow and with a sweeping thrust met the charge of the Wolf-man. The flint point entered the soft part of the belly, just below the ribs. Hunts-Well stumbled and went down, his arm still held aloft with the ax intended for Bear Paws. He could clearly hear the crack of the arrow shaft, shattering under the Wolf-man's weight as he struck the ground.

"This way!" called Spotted Cat.

The two hurried away, Bear Paws' right arm hanging limply. It had not yet begun to feel the pain that would come later. He followed the tracker, running along an obscure animal trail that wound through the thicket. *Aiee, can he see in the dark?* thought Bear Paws.

The tracker paused, and they looked out into a little clearing. Bear Paws recognized the place. Here was the purification fire, now abandoned. They sprinted across, down the ravine, and a horse nickered in the darkness ahead. He could see the dim forms of horses, prancing eagerly, excited from the excitement they perceived in the horsemen.

"Your horse, Strong Bow," said Running Otter, handing the rein.

"Help him up," the tracker said shortly. "He is hurt."

He started to protest, but realized that there was no way in which he could mount the stallion alone. Running Otter took the rein back again, and Spotted Cat helped him to the saddle.

Tall Bull and Calling Bird, who had been talking excitedly in each other's arms, now separated. They quickly mounted their horses . . . Cat had selected a well-muscled gray mare for the girl. Running Otter led the way, and the others followed, the tracker bringing up the rear.

"We must gain some distance before they follow," Otter called back over his shoulder.

He settled into an easy, ground-eating lope. They must save the horses as much as possible, because the loss of even one animal might easily be fatal to the whole party.

It was growing light, now. Open plains stretched ahead. Bear Paws could not believe that they had actually made it happen. His injured arm was throbbing, but it did not seem to matter. There was no blood, so it was not an ax wound. They could examine it later. He did not seem to feel the grating sensation that would indicate a broken bone.

It was good . . . the day was good, the world. They had succeeded. He was pleased that there had been no more bloodshed. He had worried that he might have to kill someone he knew. Red Hand . . . *aiee*, a friend indeed!

How clever, to hold the others back while pretending to try to kill him! He had not had time to thank his friend, or even say good-bye. But Red Hand would know.

Hunts-Well was dead. There was no question of that. Were there any others? He thought not. The man whose groin must still ache would recover . . . the one whose neck and ear would bear the burns of the torch . . . It was strange to worry about the injuries of the enemy, but this was different. These were people who had been his people for the past few seasons. The people of his wife's tribe.

Only then, as that thought struck him, did the finality of this morning's events strike home. He could never go back. He wondered if Pretty Sky would have any regrets. She might merely be glad to be rid of him.

After some distance, Running Otter called a pause to let the horses blow. They continued at a walk. Spotted Cat fell behind to watch for signs of pursuit.

"How goes it with you, Strong Bow?" Otter asked.

"It is not bad," he answered. It was quite good, actually, to be called by his own name.

"Is anyone else hurt?" Running Otter inquired. There was no reply.

Calling Bird was stripping the remaining fragments of buckskin from her wrists and tossing them aside.

"*Aiee,*" she said, "how good to see all of you. I thought I was dead!"

"I do not see . . ." began Tall Bull, but Running Otter waved him to silence.

"Later, Bull."

Calling Bird was looking at her rescuer with a puzzled expression.

"You are . . . Strong Bow, my brother said? You are not a Horn-man?"

"No. I am of the People."

"Then how . . . why . . . ?"

Strong Bow smiled.

"Who knows? I was meant to help you, maybe."

"You have lived with them? The Horn People?"

"Yes. But now, I go home."

She laughed, and her laughter was like the song of birds in the Moon of Roses.

"It is good. I, too, go home! I thank you. I do not understand it all . . ."

"None of us does," he answered. "But we do go home."

"Which is your band?"

"The Southern."

She nodded.

"Ours is the Northern band."

"Yes, I know. The others told me."

"Oh . . . yes, of course. You have spoken with them."

"Yes, we planned this together."

Tall Bull seemed a little jealous over their conversation, and reined in on the other side of the gray mare. Strong Bow decided to leave the young lovers alone. He kicked his horse forward to join Running Otter.

"Aiee!" he said softly. "That part is over!"

Otter nodded.

"Well you have said 'that part,' my brother! We are far from home, and they are sure to follow."

"Yes, I am made to think so. Are your horses strong?" He had no doubts about his own black.

"Yes. If we have problems we will trade or steal more as we travel."

"It is good."

It was much later, after extensive observation of their back trail, that Spotted Cat rejoined them and made a startling announcement.

"We are not followed."

Strong Bow met this statement with mixed feelings. It was good, of course, that there was no immediate pursuit. However . . .

"It is good, so far," he cautioned. "But it means only one thing. They are taking a little time to form a war party."

23

>> >> >>

They made rapid progress, though pausing frequently to rest the horses. They stopped at a small stream, where Calling Bird scrubbed the painted sign of Morning Star from her forehead. This appeared to give her a great sense of relief.

"Can I get something else to wear?" she asked her brother. "I feel it is not over, while I still wear this."

She indicated the black two-piece dress that she had worn for the ceremony.

"We will see," Otter assured her. "First we must be sure of escape."

During the first night stop the girl began to talk, freeing herself of the burden of the ordeal. The others were silent, understanding that this was needed. A tiny fire pushed back the darkness. The night-sounds were pleasant, as normal as if it had not been a day of terror and death.

Spotted Cat had disappeared into the twilight as soon

as they dismounted, to watch the back trail. The horses were grazing quietly, hobbled to prevent their wandering.

Strong Bow crouched near the fire, allowing the warmth to penetrate his injured shoulder. He had removed his shirt to allow examination of the wound. He could not see it well, but Running Otter palpated it gently. A livid plum-colored bruise crossed the shoulder point over the bone, but the skin was intact. Otter moved the arm gently.

"The bone is not broken," he said in assurance. "Do your fingers move?"

Strong Bow wiggled his right hand experimentally.

"Yes . . . they do not want to, very much."

Otter laughed. "It is good! It will be slow, my friend, but we are all alive!"

Tall Bull hovered near the girl. Otter had cautioned him to go slowly, to allow her to return to reality. Just now she was sitting, staring into the fire, absently poking the glowing coals with a stick.

"At first, when I was stolen, I knew that someone would come to help me. But no one did."

"I . . ." began Tall Bull, but Otter waved him to silence. His heart was heavy, but the two lovers could discuss the matter later, in the warmth of privacy.

"They treated me well," she went on. "They protected me from harm, gave me the best of their food . . . Did you know that they killed one of their own who would have harmed me?"

"Yes, we found him," said Otter quietly.

"I had never felt so honored," the girl continued dreamily. "Is this hard to understand?"

The men shook their heads.

"Go on," said her brother.

"They made me feel very special. I was needed, the

Wolf-man said, for their most important of ceremonies."

She paused, and the others waited in silence. She stared into the heart of the glowing fire, seemingly oblivious to her surroundings.

"We talked in signs, of course," she went on. "I asked why a woman from another nation was chosen, but they said it is always so. But I was treated so well . . . the women whose task it was to care for me . . . the best of food . . . the ceremonies each day . . . I did not want it to end!

"Then this morning. My hands . . . tied! They told me that was to be sure I did not fall. Even then, I believed them. *Aiee,* I was so stupid!"

"No, no, go on!" urged her brother.

"When I saw them take out the bow and arrow, I finally knew," she admitted. "I was sure I was dead. But I prayed, and you came, all of you. It was like a dream. *Aiee,* I will never sleep well again! Maybe I will never escape."

"What do you mean?" asked Tall Bull anxiously.

"I was chosen by Morning Star," she said dreamily. "He sent them to search for me. Maybe I still belong to him."

Running Otter and Strong Bow exchanged anxious glances.

"I am made to think not," Otter said quickly.

"Maybe I should go back," she mused, still staring at the fire.

Strong Bow was alarmed. After all the risk and the planning of the rescue, this was a totally unexpected twist. Could the power of the Morning Star still be this great? He had wondered whether the girl had been drugged with a potion of some sort, but now he wondered again. Had her captors twisted her mind, some-how?

He thought back over the events of the past few days. The ceremonies in the darkness of the earth-lodge . . . What had they done to her? No one knew what sort of pressures were used to influence the spirit of the captive. The sacred star fire, burning continually for the four days . . . like this fire . . . like the red glow of the star as it crawled over Earth's rim.

She has not yet escaped! he realized. *Her spirit is still captive!*

"We should put out the fire," he said aloud, "in case we are followed."

Running Otter looked at him with surprise.

"Cat is out there to watch," he said.

"Yes, but I am made to think we should not mark our camp," insisted Strong Bow.

He rose and started pulling the fire apart.

"No . . ." Calling Bird protested feebly.

"Yes, it must be so!" he insisted.

Normally, a fire must be a necessary part of a camp, even if not needed for cooking or for warmth. It was a statement, an announcement going back to Creation, almost. To the first man who used fire, who fed and nurtured it, to declare to the spirits who inhabited the place: *Here I will be!*

Now it was considered only a polite gesture, a contact with whatever spirits might exist at one's camp site. A supplication, almost, a request for permission: *Here I wish to camp, and wish not to offend the spirits of this place.*

This situation was different. The malevolent power of Morning Star might override the spirits of the place. The girl had been conditioned to respond to the red glow of the fire in the earth-lodge, like the glow of the star. Her reverie had been rekindled by this fire as she stared at its glowing depths.

Would she ever be free of this risk, he wondered. This could be very difficult for her, for all of her life. She must live with fires for warmth, for cooking.

"Try to sleep, now," he suggested.

Soon Running Otter drew him aside.

"What is it?" he asked anxiously. "You saw something that I did not?"

Strong Bow explained quickly.

"She has been so long under this power," he finished, "that she has not yet escaped it. I am made to think that the fire made it stronger."

"*Aiee!* Is this a belief of the Horn People?"

"I do not know, but something is not right. Morning Star still has some power over her. We must watch her closely. She might even try to go back!"

"The star is *that* powerful?"

"The Horn People think so. If your sister believes it, it is true."

"*Aiee!* We must be careful!"

"Yes. When we get back to the People, maybe a holy man can help us. My brother, Red Horse, has knowledge of such things."

"It is good. I will tell Tall Bull what we suspect. He must not push her too fast. She might feel forced to choose between him and her Star-spirit!"

It was a totally unexpected thing, and quite uncomfortable to think about, because of its unknown qualities. It was no less so when Spotted Cat returned some time later.

"There is something strange," he said. "We are not followed."

"Then that is good!" answered Otter.

He and Strong Bow were awake, still talking while Tall Bull and the girl slept.

"Maybe," admitted the tracker, "but I am not sure. I am made to wonder why. *Why are we not followed?*"

A doubt gripped the heart of Strong Bow. Was this part of the same, the strange power of Morning Star? Was the Morning Star Priest so secure in his power that no pursuit was *needed?* Did the priest know that the girl would somehow return by her own choosing? His skin crawled at such a thought.

"Why did you kill the fire?" the tracker asked.

They explained the strange reaction of the girl.

"Do you really think this?" asked Spotted Cat.

"You did not see my sister, Cat," said Otter seriously. "I was made to think so."

"And you? Do you know something of this?" he asked Strong Bow.

"No. Only what we saw. But we both . . . Otter and I . . . felt that she might even try to go back."

"*Aiee!* Really?"

"Cat, this is strong spirit-medicine," said Otter. "We must watch her carefully. She *spoke* that maybe she still belongs to Morning Star!"

Spotted Cat thought for a moment and finally spoke, a sense of awe in his voice.

"Is this why we are not followed? They do not need to follow, because she will go back when she has the chance?" He looked at Strong Bow. "Is their holy man this powerful?"

"I do not know. The Horn People do whatever he says. One of them had a vision, to go and find a bride for Morning Star."

"They came all the way to our Sacred Hills to find this girl?"

"Yes, so they said."

Spotted Cat sank to a squatting position, half-lost in thought.

"Aiee," he murmured, "this is great power!"

Strong Bow was not pleased with the way this conversation was going.

"But we have beaten him once," he pointed out. "We took the girl from him."

He was thinking of the morning on the hill, when he had shaken his weapon at the glowing red eye on the eastern rim of earth. It had felt good, and he had proved that Morning Star could be defied. He could not have explained all of this to his companions, but he knew that it was true. He had challenged Morning Star and had won. Had won that battle, anyway. The girl had been saved.

Was there to be yet another confrontation? Could Morning Star yet defeat them?

He was tired, his shoulder in pain. He had hardly slept for two days. His body had been crying out for rest as they traveled, and he had looked forward to sleep. Now he feared it was not to be. Not yet. He must be alert to the ongoing danger that followed them.

Of one thing he was certain. He *had* challenged and won, so he could again. This thought stirred a determination, an anger in him that caused a rush of energy through his tired limbs. Even his injured shoulder did not throb as much.

He wrapped in his robe and lay down to rest, though he doubted that he would sleep.

"Morning Star," he whispered to the unseen spirit in the dark heavens, *"I am still here!"*

24

>> >> >>

Next morning Calling Bird seemed to have recovered from the effects of the incident by the campfire. She was cheerful and active, and once more seemed to have put the events of her captivity behind her. Repeatedly, she expressed her thanks for deliverance.

Strong Bow and Running Otter were not quite convinced. She had appeared this way yesterday as they traveled, too. There must have been something about the darkness after night fell, and the glowing red of the fire . . . But she seemed to have slept well. The others had done so, too, giving in to the sleep of exhaustion and the letdown after the excitement of escape.

They had taken turns at watch through the night. Spotted Cat was still troubled over the lack of pursuit.

"We should have been followed!" he insisted. "If a few strangers interrupted our Sun Dance and destroyed its meaning, we would hunt them down. The warrior societies would think that the most important task of the season."

It was true, and they could not understand it.

"They have no warrior societies like ours," said Strong Bow, "but this is most unlike them. I thought they would follow us."

He thought of his friend Red Hand. That had been a brave thing, for him to secretly help with the escape. Could there be others, not completely sure about the grisly human sacrifice, who had now spoken out? But the power of Hawk's Tail, the Morning Star Priest, seemed so great. He had completely influenced the total activity of the Horn People for a season.

"We must continue to watch closely," he suggested. "They may still come after us."

Spotted Cat agreed. He took it on himself to see that the back trail was safe, waiting behind, riding back, scouting at night. Still he reported nothing.

They also took the precaution of watching the girl closely. She was never left alone, especially at night. They took care not to let her gaze into the glowing coals of the night-fire, for that had seemed to bring on her strange depression.

At the first opportunity, they stopped at a village of Growers. The cut of their garments was different from those of the People, but Calling Bird did not seem to mind. She eagerly exchanged the black ceremonial dress for a buckskin shirt and trousers such as a man might wear.

"*Aiee,* I never want to see that dress again," she said with relief.

Strong Bow felt better about it, too. He suspected that the dress itself might affect the girl's thoughts.

It was also at this stop that he acquired the yucca suds to wash the paint and tallow out of his own hair. He would no longer be a Horn-man. His appearance was ludicrous, of course. The unshaved hair of the "horn," now loose and falling in all directions, contrasted with the new stubble of his shaved head. The others roared with laughter.

"Aiee, you are more frightening than before!" laughed Running Otter.

Strong Bow smiled ruefully.

"It took a long time to become a Horn-man," he admitted. "It may take a while to undo it."

"No, no. You are a man of the People, now," Calling Bird assured him. "Did you not save me?"

They had traveled four days when Spotted Cat returned from one of his scouting forays. There was a strange, puzzled look on his face.

"We are followed now," he said solemnly.

"How many?" asked Otter.

"I saw only two. But they may be the wolves of a bigger party. You go on, and I will find out. Something is not quite right."

"What do you mean?" asked Strong Bow.

"I do not know. They do not ride as our wolves do, but together. Is that their way, Strong Bow?"

"No . . . let me go back with you. Maybe we can tell more."

"It is good. Come." He turned to Otter. "Go on ahead, and we will join you tonight." He started to mount, but then turned again. "If we do not, push on faster," he advised.

Running Otter nodded soberly.

They rode swiftly across the rolling country. The tracker seemed to know exactly where he was going.

"Here," he said briefly, turning aside into a clump of

trees. They muzzled the horses, and Cat led the way to a slight rise.

Strong Bow realized that the tracker had already made his plans. Where to hide the horses, the point from which to observe . . . Once more he was impressed by Cat's skilled efficiency.

"We watch from here," said the tracker as they approached the crest of the low hillock. "They will be there."

He pointed to the north.

The two men crawled the last few steps and peered between the woody stems of sumac. A grassy plain stretched before them, the plain over which they had been traveling. It was laced with ribbons of darker green, the trees along the watercourses and small streams. It took a few moments to scan the panorama and pick out the figures that had caught the attention of Spotted Cat.

They were nearer than he had expected, but still far off. Far enough, in fact, that he could not distinguish the color of the horses. That had always been a wonder to him, the way in which at a distance all things become the same color. Motion can be seen, and even individual animals can be distinguished, much farther than their colors can. A horse at this distance might be red or bay, but just as easily yellow, spotted, even black or white, and the watcher could not tell.

"See, they ride together," the tracker said. "At first I thought a pair of deer, maybe. But see, they come straight this way. They follow us."

"Are you sure? Maybe they only travel this same direction."

"Maybe. But we cannot risk it. We lost a day at the Growers' town, and they could overtake us now. Do you see any others? A main war party?"

"No . . . this is strange, Cat. Should we go back to see them closer?"

"No. Let them use up their horses, while ours rest." The tracker rolled over onto his back and lay there, completely relaxed. "Wake me when they are closer," he said.

Strong Bow was amused. He had wondered how this man could continue to travel, as well as scout, day and night, without rest. This was the answer. He was a person who could rest, maybe even sleep a little while, at any time, anywhere. It was a gift, as his tracking skills were a gift.

Strong Bow watched the two horsemen draw slowly nearer. It was near mid-afternoon, and it appeared that those who followed them would reach this spot well before dark. Their progress was not rapid, actually, but methodical. Plodding, almost. And certainly, they were not outriders for a war party. He had decided that by the time Spotted Cat awoke.

The tracker glanced at the sun's position and at that of the riders.

"Ah, they are closer. You have seen no others?"

"No, they are alone."

"I see . . . Strong Bow, I feel that we must know. Yet, we must tell the others there is no danger yet. Will you go on, and tell them?"

"Of course. What will you do?"

"Watch these who follow. I will come close to their camp after dark, and then come to join you."

It was late when the tracker approached their camp. *"Ah-koh,"* he called, "it is Spotted Cat!"

He was chuckling as he dismounted.

"That is a woman, Strong Bow. A woman of the Horn

People, from her dress. The other horse carries two children. I thought for a while it was a pack horse."

"A *woman?*" Strong Bow asked in amazement.

"Yes. I do not understand this. I think she follows us. Why would this be so? Maybe you should come back with me to see them."

The two were well hidden the next morning when the woman approached, her horse followed by the other, carrying the children.

"Sky!" muttered Strong Bow.

"What?"

"Pretty Sky . . . that is my wife!"

"Your *wife?*"

Strong Bow was already on his feet and running forward. Sky started to rein her horse away, but then recognized him, and stood waiting for his approach.

"Sky . . . what are you doing here?"

"I follow you," she said simply.

"But . . . I thought you would choose a new husband!"

"You are my husband. I chose you," she stated simply. But, there was doubt in her face. "If you want me . . ."

"Of course . . . but I stopped the ceremony. Your Morning Star."

Pretty Sky shrugged. She looked tired, but he had never seen her more beautiful. He longed to hold her.

"That was meant to be," she told him. "Hawk's Tail said that it was the fault of Hunts-Well, who had a false vision."

"But how . . . ?"

"Many did not believe it," she went on. "Some were glad . . . Red Hand said to tell you it is good."

"He helped me."

"I know. I saw. But the power of Hawk's Tail is weakened. His sacred arrow was broken. He said it is the will of Morning Star. That is why you were not followed."

He stood there, numbly, trying to realize what this implied. The strange spell over Calling Bird would be broken. Pretty Sky was here . . .

"Will you come with me to my people?" he asked.

She slid from the horse and into his arms, wetting his chest with her tears.

"I was afraid you would not want me," she whispered. "You have been so distant."

He was astonished. *She* had been concerned that she was losing *him*. And she cared enough to leave her people and follow him into the unknown. It would have been much easier for her to remain with her people.

"But I was meant to . . . called to . . . the Morning Star Maiden!"

"I know, now," Pretty Sky said. "But I was jealous. I thought you wanted her. I wanted her dead."

"No . . . she has a husband-to-be."

Sky smiled, a smile with some degree of relief.

"It is good," she said through her tears.

He folded her tightly in his arms.

"This is good," he whispered.

"Come, we should travel," said the tracker.

"Yes, that is true. Sky, this is Spotted Cat. He is . . . well, I will tell you later, all of it."

He turned to give the children a quick hug while Pretty Sky remounted her horse. Then he stepped back to his big black and swung up.

Pretty Sky was giggling.

"What happened to your hair?" she asked, teasing him.

And it was good.

GENEALOGY

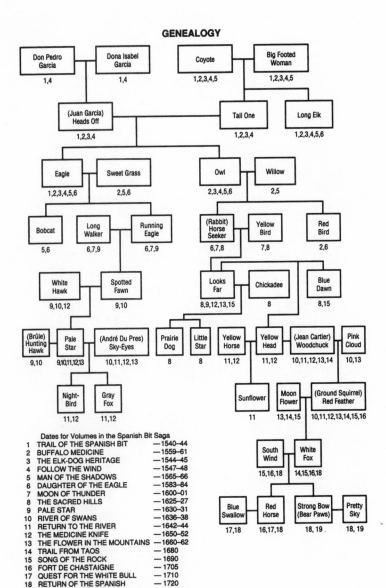

Don Pedro Garcia — 1,4 — Dona Isabel Garcia — 1,4
Coyote — 1,2,3,4,5 — Big Footed Woman — 1,2,3,4,5
(Juan Garcia) Heads Off — 1,2,3,4 — Tall One — 1,2,3,4 — Long Elk — 1,2,3,4,5,6
Eagle — 1,2,3,4,5,6 — Sweet Grass — 2,5,6 — Owl — 2,3,4,5,6 — Willow — 2,5
Bobcat — 5,6 — Long Walker — 6,7,9 — Running Eagle — 6,7,9 — (Rabbit) Horse Seeker — 6,7,8 — Yellow Bird — 7,8 — Red Bird — 2,6
White Hawk — 9,10,12 — Spotted Fawn — 9,10 — Looks Far — 8,9,12,13,15 — Chickadee — 8 — Blue Dawn — 8,15
(Brûle) Hunting Hawk — 9,10 — Pale Star — 9,10,11,12,13 — (André Du Pres) Sky-Eyes — 10,11,12,13 — Prairie Dog — 8 — Little Star — 8 — Yellow Horse — 11,12 — Yellow Head — 11,12 — (Jean Cartier) Woodchuck — 10,11,12,13,14 — Pink Cloud — 10,13
Night-Bird — 11,12 — Gray Fox — 11,12 — Sunflower — 11 — Moon Flower — 13,14,15 — (Ground Squirrel) Red Feather — 10,11,12,13,14,15,16
South Wind — 15,16,18 — White Fox — 14,15,16,18
Blue Swallow — 17,18 — Red Horse — 16,17,18 — Strong Bow (Bear Paws) — 18,19 — Pretty Sky — 18,19

Dates for Volumes in the Spanish Bit Saga

1	TRAIL OF THE SPANISH BIT	—1540–44
2	BUFFALO MEDICINE	—1559–61
3	THE ELK-DOG HERITAGE	—1544–45
4	FOLLOW THE WIND	—1547–48
5	MAN OF THE SHADOWS	—1565–66
6	DAUGHTER OF THE EAGLE	—1583–84
7	MOON OF THUNDER	—1600–01
8	THE SACRED HILLS	—1625–27
9	PALE STAR	—1630–31
10	RIVER OF SWANS	—1636–38
11	RETURN TO THE RIVER	—1642–44
12	THE MEDICINE KNIFE	—1650–52
13	THE FLOWER IN THE MOUNTAINS	—1660–62
14	TRAIL FROM TAOS	—1680
15	SONG OF THE ROCK	—1690
16	FORT DE CHASTAIGNE	—1705
17	QUEST FOR THE WHITE BULL	—1710
18	RETURN OF THE SPANISH	—1720
19	BRIDE OF THE MORNING STAR	—1725

Dates are only approximate, since the People have no written calendar.
Characters in the Genealogy appear in the volumes indicated.

Don Coldsmith was born in Iola, Kansas, in 1926. He served as a World War II combat medic in the South Pacific and returned to his native state, where he graduated from Baker University in 1949 and received his M.D. from the University of Kansas in 1958. He worked at several jobs before entering medical school: He was a YMCA Youth Director, a gunsmith, a taxidermist, and for a short time a Congregational preacher. In addition to his private medical practice, Dr. Coldsmith has been a staff physician at Emporia State University's Health Center, where he also teaches in the English Department. He discontinued medical pursuits in 1990 to devote more time to his writing. He and his wife Edna, of thirty years, operate a small cattle ranch. They have raised five daughters.

Dr. Coldsmith produced the first ten novels in the Spanish Bit Saga in a five-year period; he writes and revises the stories first in his head, then in longhand. From this manuscript the finished version is skillfully typed by his longtime secretary.

Of his decision to create, or re-create, the world of the Plains Indian in the early centuries of European contact, the author says: "There has been very little written about this time period. I wanted also to portray these Native Americans as human beings, rather than as stereotyped 'Indians.' That word does not appear anywhere in the series, for a reason. As I have researched the time and place, the indigenous cultures, it's been a truly inspiring experience for me."